Dancing Queen

Text copyright © 2008 by Cathy Hopkins
Cover illustration copyright © 2008 by Monica Laiter
KINGFISHER
Published in the United States by Kingfisher,
an imprint of Henry Holt and Company LLC,
175 Fifth Avenue, New York, New York 10010.
First published in Great Britain by Kingfisher Publications plc,
an imprint of Macmillan Children's Books, London.

Distributed in Canada by H. B. Fenn and Company Ltd.

Library of Congress Cataloging-in-Publication Data
has been applied for.

ISBN: 978-0-7534-6296-6

Kingfisher books are available for special promotions and premiums.
For details contact: Director of Special Markets, Holtzbrinck Publishers.

First American Paperback Edition April 2009
Printed in the United Kingdom by
CPI Mackays, Chatham ME5 8TD
10 9 8 7 6 5 4 3 2 1
1TR/0109/MCK/(SC)/60HLM/C

Dancing Queen

Cathy Hopkins

KINGFISHER
NEW YORK

Chapter One

Hairtastic

"You're not really going to do it, are you?" asked Lois, after Mom had finally left for the grocery store and Lois and I were alone in the house. I nodded as we watched Mom through the window in the hallway. She struggled with her umbrella against the October rain, closed the gate, got into the car, and drove off.

I punched the air. "Let's move," I said. "We only have three hours before the auditions."

Lois gave me a salute, and then we raced along to the bathroom, where I locked the door just in case Mom came back for any reason.

I handed Lois the rubber gloves and the bleach that I'd been hiding in a plastic bag in my backpack for the last few days. "Here. Hold these while I wet my hair. And don't worry. I called Mom's hairdresser, and she gave me very clear instructions. All I have to do is bleach my color out, which might take a couple of applications, then put on a toner, and bingo: white hair."

"But, Marsha, your lovely red hair," she objected.

1

"What if it goes green or something?"

I laughed. "I'll deal with it. Everyone's always saying that we should 'go green' these days."

"That's not what I meant, dingbat brain. And where's your dad? What if he turns up?"

"Chill, Lois. He plays football every Saturday morning, and both my sisters are out with friends. It will be fine. Trust me. I'm not going green—I'm going white."

Through the mirror to my left, I saw Lois glance at me anxiously. We made a strange pair. Lois with her long, straight blond hair and me with my shoulder-length red curls that, try as I might, always looked unruly. I looked like an urchin with a petulant face standing next to a princess with dreamy eyes. "Red hair is not right for the part, and I have to get that part."

Lois sighed and sat on the edge of the bathtub. She knew better than to argue with me when I wanted something, and I wanted the part of the Ice Queen in the school play badly.

"Why is it so important to bleach your hair?" she asked.

"Don't you know anything?" I asked. "If an actor is serious about a role, they have to live and breathe the part, tap into their secret self, dredge up old experiences to make it real. It's called method acting."

"Since when have you had any experience being an Ice Queen?"

"Hmm. I suppose I haven't, but . . . I can imagine what it would be like to be an Ice Queen; I guess that's the next best thing."

"And bleaching your hair white is method acting?"

"Methodish. It's like some actors put on weight or lose it for a part. I'm trying to become my character so that it will be more than acting. She will be an extension of myself. Like a part of me."

Lois rolled her eyes. "But you won't have to act. All you have to do is dance." She laughed and added, "and lure Oliver Blake . . ."

"Swoon, swoon," I said. One of us always said that whenever anyone mentioned Oliver's name. He's the school babe and is totally hunky.

". . . into your arms," Lois continued. "That's really why you want the role, isn't it?"

"Only partly," I said. I did have a crush on Oliver, but then so did the whole school, and I knew he would think that a girl in seventh grade was way too young for him. "It's also a way of being in the play and having an excuse to hang around with the drama group and, yeah, you're right, Oliver, swoon . . ."

"Swoon," we chorused.

". . . without having to kill myself or learn loads of

lines. You know how I get bored so easily." (Or have no staying power, as my mom would say.)

"Unlike some of us," said Lois, who was going for a speaking part and had spent the best part of last week memorizing huge chunks of the play. "I don't get it. You've never been that interested in being in a play before."

"Yeah, but that was before I realized that I want to be in the entertainment business."

Lois rolled her eyes to the ceiling again. "I thought you wanted to be an Olympic gymnast."

"That was last week."

"No. Last week you wanted to be a champion tennis player."

"No. That was the week before. A girl can change her mind, can't she? In fact, ours is the age for dipping in and trying different things—our teachers say that all the time. And this week I am utterly convinced that I want to be on the stage."

There was another reason that I wanted the part, though. Word had been going around school that Oliver's parents would be attending: Mr. and Mrs. Blake. But I was most interested in Mr. Blake. Everyone at our school knew who he was. Michael Blake, agent to the stars. He was Mr. Show Business and could make or break a person's career. Hearing that he was going to be there is what swung wanting to be in the play for me. It could be the steppingstone to a whole new life. A life of glamour and fame. Oliver was already a celebrity. He had been an extra in three Christmas blockbuster movies, and he even had a line to say in the last one. As soon as I heard that, I knew I had to go for it. I was born to be famous. Everyone says so, not just me.

I followed Katie's instructions to the letter, and the last part was to apply the toner and then wait.

"Fifteen minutes," I said. "A quick blow dry and then we can go."

"Okay, then let's look at our horoscopes while we wait," Lois suggested. "Maybe it will tell us if we're going to get parts in the play. I found a really good website last night. Open your computer, and I'll show you."

Lois was always trying out New Age–type things like astrology and fortune telling. She says it's because she's an Aquarian and they are into stuff like that. I'm not convinced by it, but it can be fun to read my horoscope, especially if it says something good.

"Good idea," I said. "Let's see what the stars have to say."

We went into my room, where I turned on my laptop and made room for Lois to sit at my desk by the window. I stretched and yawned before flopping onto my bed and kicking one of the turquoise cushions onto the floor.

5

"God, I wish we could move sometimes. This house is so small!"

"No, it's not," said Lois. "Your mom and dad have made it really cozy here, and I love your room since you painted it pale blue." I knew that she was only being polite. She lived in an enormous old house with high ceilings and large square rooms—her family even had two bathrooms, one with a bathtub and one with a shower, and they had a kitchen area at the back that opened out onto an enclosed porch. I loved going there; it felt so light and spacious. With five of us living here, our house felt like we were all squashed in. We had only one bathroom, which drove me crazy when there was a line (which there usually was in the morning). I wished Mom and Dad would move, but they seemed happy with little rooms and what they call a galley kitchen at the back downstairs. Personally, I am made for bigger, better things, and one day the world will realize this.

Lois typed in the Web address.

"Who first?" she asked.

"Me me me," I said. "I can't wait to find out what it says."

A page showing a starry night sky came into view and then a form asking for time of birth, date of birth, and place.

"Born here," I said. "April second, seven-fifteen in the

6

morning. I remember because Mom always moans that I kept her awake all night."

Lois typed in my name and my details, and seconds later the laptop began to shake like a cell phone on the vibrate setting. The screen began to glow and then looked like it had burst into flames with red, orange, and yellow flickers of fire dancing in front of our eyes.

"Wow!" I exclaimed.

"Ohmigod, sorry," said Lois, who didn't look impressed. She looked worried. "I . . . I must have pressed something wrong."

Suddenly, out of the fire, a golden banner appeared with a message saying, "Congratulations, Marsha! You are this month's Zodiac Girl!"

"Oh!" said Lois. "What's this all about?"

"Meeee. Yea! I'm a Zodiac Girl." I leaped up and did a karate-type kick into the air. "Huzzah."

Lois laughed, and I looked back at the screen, where a second banner appeared, saying, "As an Aries, your sign is ruled by the planet Mars." Music began to play, drums and then trumpets rising in volume and getting so loud that Lois put her hands over her ears.

"Turn it down," she said, and I leaned over her and attempted to turn down the volume, but it didn't appear to work—the loud music continued.

"Oh, phooey, never mind all the fancy schmancy

stuff," I said. "What do I win?"

A third banner appeared, saying, "As a typical Aries, you are always in a hurry to move on to the next best thing . . ."

Lois laughed. "That's true," she said, as I continued reading the screen.

"Slow down or else Uranus, who features strongly in your chart at the beginning of this month, will steer you in an unexpected direction." I glanced farther down the screen. "Nothing about winning a major role in a play? Or . . . hold on, here's another part."

"As this month's Zodiac Girl," it continued on the screen, "this could be the most special four weeks of your entire life. A turning point. Your guardian will contact you. Make of it what you will."

"Guardian? What guardian? What's that about?" I asked.

Lois shrugged. "Don't know."

"Ooh, spooky," I said and put on my Russian spy accent. "Make of eet vot you vill. This is a strange site, Lois."

"I know. It's weird. It certainly didn't do that when I looked before. Maybe it's a promotion or something to bring in more users. Website designers are always looking for new tricks."

"Yeah, but hey. The most special four weeks of my life?

A turning point? That has to mean the play, doesn't it? I think it's a really good forecast."

"But what about the Zodiac Girl thing?" asked Lois.

I shrugged. "Dunno. You're the astrology expert."

"Not really. I think it's something like you were the thousandth person to type in your details. If we'd done me first, it would be telling me that I'm a Zodiac Girl."

"That's what I think," I said. "Do yours, do yours."

Lois typed in her details. Moments later, the page showed a horoscope, but there were no banners or music. "This month looks set to be a busy time, and creative urges are strong now. Keep yourself focused and make time to recharge. Duh. How boring is that?"

"Anything else?" I asked. Then, "A time for change: go shopping or get a new pet," I read off the screen.

Lois shrugged. "I was thinking of getting another goldfish, so I guess it's accurate enough. But you are so lucky, Marsha. All the good things happen to you."

I smiled. "I know. I am lucky. And I feel in my bones that this is going to be an amazing time." I stood up as straight as I could and lifted my right arm up and pointed out of the window and up at the sky. "I AM ZODIAC GIRL. Hiii-YAH!" I did another karate-type kick. "Mess with me, and you mess with the PLANETS!" I chopped at the air around me. "Hoi. Hoi. HOI."

Lois glanced at her watch. "Oops. It's time, Marsha."

"Ohmigod. I hope my hair's turned out okay." We raced to the bathroom, and I began to rinse off the toner. Halfway through the process, there was a loud knocking on the door.

"Oh no!" said Lois. "We've been rumbled."

"Who is it?" I asked in my best casual voice.

"The bogeyman!" my sister Cissie called back. "Hurry up, you idiot. I need the bathroom, and so does Eleanor. Get a move on. Sandy's dad is waiting in the car for us outside."

"Can't, I'm busy," I said.

"You've got two seconds, Marsha," Eleanor called, "or your life won't be worth living. What are you doing in there, anyway?"

"Nothing," said Lois.

"So let us in," said Eleanor.

"I'd better open the door," I said, "or else they might cause trouble." I quickly pulled a towel over my head and unlocked the bathroom door. Cissie and Eleanor were standing there, looking annoyed and suspicious. They always look at me like that—it's part of the price I pay for being the youngest sister.

"Yes. What were you doing in here, kid?" asked Cissie, as Eleanor shoved past her.

"Um. Hair wash and then we're doing makeovers, and

don't call me kid," I said.

"Okay, kid," said Cissie. I wanted to punch her but resisted because I wanted her to go.

"You have great hair," said Lois, putting her hand up to touch Cissie's long red locks, which she was wearing loose down her back. "You three are so lucky. I wish my hair was such a gorgeous color." *Good tactic*, I thought, as Lois gushed on about the Leibowitz family's red hair. All three of us girls have inherited it from Mom, and Cissie was a sucker for flattery.

Eleanor wasn't long in the bathroom and flew straight down the stairs without even giving us a second glance, and then Cissie went in. Loud beeping from their friend Sandy's dad's car horn on the road outside prevented Cissie from hanging around too long either, so minutes later we were back in the bathroom.

"Phew," I said. "That was close."

"I know," said Lois. She looked worried. "You've had the toner on around ten minutes longer than you should have."

"It will be okay," I said and leaned over the bath so that I could rinse my hair. Once done, I toweled my hair and then looked in the mirror.

"Wow!" said Lois.

"Superyummingdoopah!" I gasped. My hair looked amazing. Katie's advice had worked perfectly, and my hair

11

was as white as snow. The texture felt a little brittle, probably because of the two applications of bleach, but overall it was a great result.

"It makes your eyes look so blue, even bluer than before," said Lois. "And it makes your skin look really pale. Perfect for the Ice Queen."

I nodded and then ran some gel through so my hair slicked right back off my face. As I did so, a few strands of hair came out. "Oops," I said as I put them in the garbage. So I'd lost a few strands of hair. The effect was perfect. It not only looked cool but also made me look like I was from another planet.

Mom was going to kill me.

Chapter Two

Star student

"I'm at the back," I said to Lois after we'd signed in with the drama teacher, Mr. Sanderson, in the gym where the auditions were being held. He had taken our names and directed us to different areas that were already filling up with eager wannabes. Dancers at the back of the hall, speaking parts up on the stage, scenery people and technicians to the left, costumes to the right.

"Laters," said Lois, and she took off in the direction of the stage.

Mrs. Pierson, our gym teacher, was waiting for us at the back and smiled when she saw me—I am one of her favorite students, and gym is one of my best subjects. I sometimes wonder if gym is her best subject, though, because she doesn't look like she does much of it. She is a small, stocky lady with an enormous chest and thick legs, and if she moves too quickly, she gets out of breath. With her were six girls from eighth and ninth grade. I gave them a wave, and a couple of them smiled and waved back. Most of them looked nervous, even though we'd had a run through of the routine last week one night after school.

"What happened to your hair?" Mrs. Pierson asked.

"I did it for the part. It will wash out easy," I lied.

"That's the attitude. I like to see that my girls have tried to get into role."

One of the girls from eighth grade smiled weakly at me. She looked like she was going to throw up.

"I wish I'd thought of that," said another one of the girls.

"Now, let's get started," said Mrs. Pierson when it became clear that there weren't going to be any more contenders. She turned to the CD player on the table behind her. "We'll go alphabetically, so that means Grace Anderson—you're up first."

A small girl with long, dark hair tied back in a braid got up, and when Mrs. Pierson turned on the CD player, a piece of classical music began to play, and Grace began to go through the routine. She messed up a few steps and then lost her timing, so Mrs. Pierson turned off the music and let her begin again, but it was clear that she wasn't going to get the part. She was way too ungraceful. I quickly assessed who else was up and saw that all their names came before mine in the alphabet, which meant that I would be the last one to audition. *Excellent*, I thought, *that means I can watch what the others do, and it also gives me a chance to see the routine over and over so by the time it is my turn, I should know it really well.* To my side, I could see Carol Kennedy watching Grace and counting the steps under her breath. Carol would be my main competitor. She did ballet out of school, and everyone knew that she was a good dancer. I used to do ballet in elementary school but got bored with it after a few years and let it go when I got to middle school and got into playing more competitive sports instead. However, when I began to learn the routine for the play, I was surprised by how easily the steps came back.

After Grace was Mary. I had to stop myself from giggling because she had no sense of timing or rhythm. *This is like watching auditions for* American Idol, I thought, as Mary almost tripped over her own feet.

After Mary was Phoebe, who was okay but not really Ice Queen material. There was something about her that was too timid. After her was Ellie the goth and then Tara. Tara was pretty good, the best so far.

"Carol. You're next," said Mrs. Pierson, and Carol got to her feet, took up first position, and went into the routine. I had to admit that she danced gracefully, as light as a feather. *How can I make my audition stand out?* I asked myself as I watched her pirouette around the gym. What would mark me out as the Ice Queen above the others? I thought about what I knew about the play so far. It had been written by a boy in the 12th grade named James O'Malley, and the dance sequence was to be in the second act when the main character, played by Ollie (swoon, swoon), gets stranded in a forest in the winter in the snow. As he battles on, his life slips away, and he falls into a trance and dreams of an Ice Queen and her princesses who try to lure him to his death. A little like how mermaids used to try to lure sailors to their death in some legends. It's a totally dramatic story, and I couldn't help but think that Carol's performance, although good, was too lightweight. She looked like a fairy princess who wouldn't harm a fly.

Carol finished, and the other girls clapped. She flushed a little and smiled at them. *It ain't over yet*, I thought, as Mrs. Pierson called me to go next.

I took up first position as Carol had done and breathed deeply into my abdomen the way that I'd been taught when I used to do ballet. Stand tall, I told myself. Remember that you're a queen. And not just any queen, you are the Ice Queen with a heart that is cold and cruel.

I went into the routine, and as I did, I narrowed my eyes and glared at Mrs. Pierson and the other girls as if they were beneath me and I was thinking about killing them. *My heart is full of icicles*, I thought, as I danced and tried to convey that I was dangerous as well as queenly.

"And a one, two, three, excellent, lovely," cooed Mrs.

Pierson as the music came to an end. As they had for Carol, the girls clapped for me. I noticed that Carol didn't clap, though. She gave me a fake smile when I glanced over at her.

"That was so cool," said Phoebe. "You looked scary. Like, in control but there was an air of don't mess with me."

"Good," I said, "because that's what I was going for."

Mrs. Pierson clapped her hands. "Now, class," she said, "I want you all to watch Marsha Leibowitz and then do the routine exactly the way she does it, and then I will decide who gets the part." She gave me a nod and a smile. "Go ahead, Marsha dear."

I went through the routine again, and soon after the others copied me, and I could see Carol narrowing her eyes and glaring with all her might. But instead of looking evil, she looked as if she had just sucked a lemon.

After we'd done the routine again, Mrs. Pierson clapped her hands again. "Okay, girls. I have made my decision. Marsha Leibowitz, you shall be our Ice Queen, and Carol, Tara, and Phoebe the princesses. Mary, Ellie, and Grace, I am sure we can find you something to do. So rehearsals start next Wednesday after school." She glanced in my direction and gave me a wink.

There were a few sighs of disappointment, but Tara and Phoebe came over and congratulated me. "Thanks,"

I said. "And I'm so glad you got parts, too."

I looked over at Carol, who was staring at the floor. She didn't look up or make any comments. I shrugged and turned to leave, when Mrs. Pierson clapped her hands again. "Attention, girls in the play, hang on a second. There's someone I want you to meet."

She motioned to someone at the front of the gym, and when I turned to see who it was, I saw a tall black man wave back and begin to make his way over.

"Hubba hubba," Phoebe whispered in my ear as he got closer. He was very handsome, with a square jaw and cheekbones to die for. As he crossed the gym, everyone turned to look at him. He radiated charisma like he was a Hollywood movie star.

Mrs. Pierson flushed pink. "Girls, this is Mario Ares," she said in a strangely squeaky voice. "He's going to be working here part time and teaching some classes after school in fitness and self-defense. If any of you feel like you'd like to sign up, I think that would be an excellent idea."

Mr. Ares stared at me as if he knew me from somewhere and was trying to remember. "Ice Queen," he said.

Mrs. Pierson nodded. "And the other girls will be her princesses. Marsha is our star gym student. Aren't you, Marsha dear?"

I nodded. "It's my favorite subject."

Mr. Ares smiled. "It would be. Aries are good at sports."

"Wow! How did you know that I was an Aries?"

Mr. Ares smiled. "I'm good at spotting star signs."

"What am I?" asked Phoebe.

"Pisces," he replied and looked at the other girls. "And you two are . . . Libra and . . . Cancer."

"And me?" asked Mrs. Pierson.

"Capricorn," said Mr. Ares without a second of hesitation. He flashed her a smile. "Hard working."

Mrs. Pierson sighed. "Tell me about it. Gosh, you really have a gift for this."

"Ah, but did you know that I am not just an Aries," I said. "I am also . . ." I jumped around in a circle, ending with a karate kick. "Zodiac Girl."

"As a matter of fact, I did," said Mr. Ares.

"Yeah, right," I said. I knew he didn't. He couldn't. He was just being smart. "So what does that mean, then?"

Mr. Ares looked up over my right shoulder as if he was reading an invisible screen. "It means . . . Mars, Saturn, and Pluto are conjunct. It means you have a major life lesson to learn. Oh, and an encounter with Uranus, so that means it may come about in an unexpected way. The planet Uranus is unpredictable, to say the least." He said it with such seriousness and then looked directly into my eyes, like he was looking right into the core of me. It sent a shiver down my spine.

"Ooh. Major life lesson? Don't we all?" asked Mrs. Pierson with a giggle. "Okay, girls, on your way. And we'll see you Wednesday."

Three planets conjunct and an encounter with another. That does sound major. *Superyummingdoopah*, I thought, as I pulled my eyes away from Mr. Ares and headed for the door. Lois was still busy up on the stage, but I managed to catch her eye and gave her the thumbs-up. She gave me the thumbs-up back.

When I glanced over my shoulder, Mr. Ares was still watching me. I gave him a wave. He wasn't going to intimidate me with his intense looks and mysterious sayings.

Chapter Three

Unexpected!

As I walked out of the gym, in my mind's eye, I could see exactly how it was going to unfold. It was going to be SPECTACULAR! Opening night, an audience buzzing with anticipation, 11th-grade boys taking photos of the stars of the show for the school magazine, me me ME and Ollie being the center of attention, all my family in the front rows, Mr. Blake seeing my performance and then asking, "Who's that girl?" He'd get my number. I could feel myself getting more and more excited at the prospect of it all. *Superyummingdoopah*. Being chosen to be a Zodiac Girl was such a good omen, and this was only the beginning of my star-studded month. Luckily, the rain had stopped and the skies had brightened, reflecting my mood. I took a deep breath of the fresh air. As I continued on my way across the school playing fields and out toward the gates, I heard footsteps behind me.

"Hey, Marsha!" a voice called. I turned to see Sophie King running to catch up with me. She was in tenth grade. A large girl with frizzy, dark hair who hung out with the geeky group from her year.

"Hey," she panted when she reached me. "I . . . I . . . just have to catch my breath." *Wuff, puff,* "I . . . I heard you got the part of the Ice Queen?"

"Yeah. Yeah, I did."

"I saw you across the gym. You were great."

"Thanks, Sophie."

"Thing is, I'm organizing a charity event to be held at the end of the month, and I wondered if you could help."

"Charity? What's it for?"

"My cousin works at the hospital out near Osbury, and she's asked me to help her raise money for a recreation wing in the children's ward."

"Oh, okay. Of course." I reached into my pocket. "I . . . I'm really sorry, I don't have much money on me," I said, as I pulled out a quarter. "I could maybe give you some more next week after I've gotten my allowance.'

"No," said Sophie. "I don't want your money. I want your talent."

"*Talent?* What do you mean?"

"We need acts for the show to draw in the crowds, and when I saw you, I thought you'd be fantastic."

"Oh! Who do you have so far?"

Sophie grimaced. "Not many, to tell you the truth. In fact, only my younger brother doing a magic act, which, between you and me, is awful, and a few seventh-grade deadbeats who want to read their poetry, which is so bad it makes me want to lie on the floor and tear my hair out. That's why I'm asking you. Someone with a bit of charisma to pull in the crowds."

Although I felt flattered, I was reluctant to get involved. Most days were packed with activities: tennis on Monday, basketball on Tuesday, there would be rehearsals for the play on Wednesday evening from now on, karate on Thursday, and Friday I had to use to catch up on homework. My life was very full. "Um . . . I . . . Um, listen, Sophie, can I think about it and get back to you?"

Sophie gave me a strange look, and I realized that I must have sounded a bit snobby. "I . . . getting the part has only just happened, and I don't know what's involved yet, you know, in the way of rehearsals, in addition to Wednesdays. Timewise I will have to put in extra to make it work. And, besides, life is pretty full on at the mo."

Sophie's expression registered weariness. Even her shoulders had slumped as if she had the weight of the world on them. "Whatever," she said. "It's really hard to get anyone to do anything like this."

"I bet lots of people will want to get involved when you ask them." (*Just not me*, I thought.) "Um, let me think about it, okay?"

Sophie turned away. "Yeah, sure. Later, then."

As we continued our separate ways, I think we both

knew that I wasn't going to be taking part in her nonevent. I did feel a twinge of guilt, though, and was grateful when I went to wait at the bus stop that Lois joined me soon after. She was as excited as I was because she had gotten the part she wanted in the play, and after we'd both recounted every moment of our auditions to each other, I filled her in on Sophie's request.

"Are you going to do it?" she asked.

"Don't think so. I don't want to. My life is, like, *soooo* busy. That's okay, isn't it? I mean, she'll find people. It's, like, celebrities get millions of requests every day, and they have to pick and choose which they do and don't do."

Lois doubled over laughing. "Celebrities! Get you. It's only the school play we're in, Marsha."

"So? One day I am going to be very famous, you watch. So you may laugh, but you'll see. In the meantime I have to learn to protect my talent and not let people drain me."

"Drain you? It's a charity show! Get real."

"Ah, but you say yes to one, you say yes to them all. Anyway, I heard Savannah Macauley—"

"Who's she?"

"Duh? Don't you know anything? She's a Hollywood A-list star, as in mega. I heard her do an interview on TV. She said that she got drained by all the constant demands on her time, and she also said that she had made some bad choices in the beginning of her career by saying yes to everyone. I took note for when I hit the big time."

Lois collapsed with laughter and slid down the wall next to the bus stop as if what I'd said was so funny that she could hardly stand up. "Marsha Leibowitz, you really are something."

"I know," I said, but I gave her a big grin to show that I wasn't really full of myself. I couldn't say yes to everyone who asked me to be in their shows. I was going to be in demand, and I had to be choosy whether Lois understood or not. "I will send her a donation from my allowance."

"How very generous of you," said Lois.

"Aye thought so," I said in an English accent that sounded like a queen and made Lois laugh even more. "But isn't it great? We're both going to be in the play, and Mr. Blake will be there . . ."

A few moments later the bus came, and we spent the rest of the journey gossiping about who else had gotten parts and sharing our fantasies about the play and the after-show party and what we were going to wear. By the time I got off at my stop, I was feeling on top of the world, so I went into the drugstore to buy a candy bar to celebrate.

Mr. Singh, who ran the store, glanced up when I walked up to the counter to pay. "Hi, Marsha," he said.

"Hey, Mr. Singh," I replied.

"I'm glad you came by," he said and slipped off his

stool to reach for a package on the top shelf behind the counter. "Someone dropped off a package for you here since there was no one at your house."

"For me?"

He handed me a package wrapped in deep red paper with a white label. "Marsha Leibowitz, Zodiac Girl," it said clearly in bright red letters.

"Oh, what is it?" I asked.

"Why don't you open it and find out?" Mr. Singh replied and then turned to serve a customer who had come in behind me.

I ripped off the paper to find two small boxes inside tied with red ribbon. I opened the smallest one first. Inside was a silver chain with a tiny charm on it. On closer inspection I saw that it was a ram's head, which I knew was the symbol for the star sign of Aries. *Cute*, I thought, and I put it on immediately. Whatever was in the second parcel was wrapped in bubble wrap so it took a little while longer to unwrap.

"Wow! It's a cell phone," I said when I'd ripped off the last piece of paper. I held it up to the light. It was exquisite, with amazing colors—deep blood red and orange—like fire. On the top of the phone, above the screen, was a dark stone that looked black at first but, if you looked closely, appeared to have layers of deeper color shining through.

"Bloodstone," said Mr. Singh. "It's very beautiful. Who's it from?"

"No idea," I replied. "I think I might have won it on an astrology website."

"Lucky you," said Mr. Singh. "Should I put the wrappings in the garbage?"

I shook my head. "No, I'll take them in case there's an address for the sender so I can thank them," I said. I pocketed the phone and headed out to the sidewalk.

This really is my lucky day, I thought, as I felt the smooth surface of the new phone in my pocket next to my old one. A part in the play, a present in the mail, and a yummy candy bar. Life really doesn't get any better.

I couldn't resist. There was a knee-high wall to my right. I stepped up and, putting one foot in front of the other, I pretended that I was on a tightrope. I put my arms out to my sides the way that I had seen performers do in the circus.

"You look happy!" called a man on a bike on the other side of the road. He seemed to have appeared from nowhere. I looked over and did a double take at his strange appearance. He had spiked-up white hair, a silver lightning bolt painted on his forehead, shiny electric-blue clothes, and his "bike" wasn't a bicycle—it was a unicycle. He looked like he was going to a sci-fi costume party.

"I am happy." I grinned back at him, and the moment

our eyes met a dog barked a short distance away. Seconds later, there was the sound of a cat screeching, frantic scrabbling, and then an orange tabby cat, spitting and hissing, shot out in front of me. It sprang off the wall, down the sidewalk, and around a corner. It all happened so fast.

"Ee . . . yoh, wuh, arrgh . . ." I cried as I lost my balance. I put out my left hand to stop my fall and landed in a crumpled heap by the wall.

The man was off his unicycle and by my side like a shot. "Oops! Oh. Are you all right? Can you get up? Stupid cat. Did you see it?"

"I . . . I . . ." Something was wrong. I put my hand out to try to push myself up onto my knees, but I yowled in pain as my left wrist crumpled like the bone had turned into rubber. "I-I'm okay, but . . . I think I hurt my wrist."

"Then don't move," said the man. "Is there someone I can call?"

I nodded, and with my right hand I pulled out my usual cell phone. "It's okay. I-I'll phone my mom, but please don't go."

The man looked at me with kind eyes. "I won't leave," he said.

And then the tears came. My wrist hurt badly.

The man kneeled down next to me. "Came out of nowhere," he said as he patted my shoulder. "Most unexpected!"

Chapter Four

Spook night

"Now this is how you do the tightrope," said the man, who had introduced himself as Uri after I'd made my call to Mom.

"No!" I cried as he lifted his unicycle onto the wall and then got up and sat on the seat. "You'll fall, too."

He winked. "Me? Never. Just watch," he said, and he began to ride along the narrow edge of the wall. After a few moments, he sprang up and stood on the seat. I wanted to clap but didn't dare in case it hurt my wrist even more. It was throbbing like crazy, and I was worried that I might have broken it.

"Whoa!" I called as Uri bent over and did a handstand. "Whoa! Be careful!" He was awesome to watch. *A little crazy*, I thought, *not someone you'd expect to run into on the way home, but impressive nonetheless. I wonder who he is.* "Are you going to a costume party?"

He laughed and shook his head.

"Children's entertainer?"

He shook his head again.

"Who, then?"

"I am Uri, otherwise known as Uranus, ruler of Aquarius, planet of the unexpected."

I laughed and did a wibbly-wobbly salute with my good hand and crossed my eyes. "Yeah, right. And I'm Queen Zugula from the planet Zog. You're just being goofy."

He shrugged. "Maybe. Maybe not." He continued to ride back and forth along the wall while we waited for Mom, and I was grateful for the distraction because I found myself forgetting that I was in pain as I watched him. It wasn't long before I saw Mom's gray car coming up the street behind him, her anxious face looking out of the window on the driver's side. As soon as she spotted me, she parked the car and leaped out. She'd obviously come straight from her Pilates class without changing because she was still in her black Lycra workout outfit, and her red hair was tied up in a bun at the back of her head.

"Ohmigod!" she cried when she saw me sitting on the sidewalk. "What have you done?" She turned to Uri, who got down from the wall with his unicycle. "And who are you?"

"He's Uri, and I've hurt my—" I started, but Mom was looking at Uri's hair and then she looked back at mine. In all the commotion, I'd forgotten that my hair was as white as his. "Your hair, Marsha! WHAT have you done to your hair?" She turned back to Uri. "What have you done to my daughter?"

"Nothing! He was just passing by when I fell. He kept me company. Never mind my hair. Never mind him, Mom. I'm in pain," I groaned.

Uri nodded. "I think she needs to go to the hospital," he said and pointed at the wall. "I think she hurt her wrist."

"Oh Lord, ohmigod!" Mom kneeled down and asked me to wiggle my fingers, and when she found that I couldn't, she tried to help me up. But as I put weight on my right foot, it crumpled beneath me.

"Ow, ow, my ankle!" I yelped. I realized that I must have fallen on it and twisted it.

"Lean on me," said Mom.

"And take my arm with your good one," said Uri. It was no use. I couldn't stand up very well, and Mom looked like she was going to faint.

"I'll lift her," said Uri, and in a second his strong hands picked me up as if I was as light as a feather.

"Open the car door," he said.

Mom opened the door, and Uri positioned me gently in the front seat.

"Let me know how she is, won't you?" asked Uri, and as Mom got into the driver's seat, he looked at me and said, "Sorry, Zodiac Girl. I know it said in your chart that you had an encounter coming up with me."

"What do you mean?"

"I told you," said Uri. "I'm Uranus, the planet of the unexpected and . . . well, sometimes I don't even know what's going to happen."

"I . . . who?" I started.

"What's he talking about?" Mom interrupted as she got into the driver's seat. "Is he crazy?" She closed the door and then wound down the window. "Away you go! Shoo, you strange man."

Uri raised an eyebrow in surprise and shrugged his shoulders at me.

"No, Mom, you don't understand. He's been kind," I protested.

"So what's he going on about? Uranus? Zodiacs?" Mom asked, starting the car.

"I don't know," I replied, turning in my seat to watch Uri out the window as we drove away. *How did he know I was a Zodiac Girl?* I wound down my window with my good hand. "How did you know I was a Zodiac Girl?" I called back to him.

But it was too late. Uri was mouthing something, but I couldn't hear above the roar of the engine, and seconds later the car turned a corner and my mystery companion had disappeared.

Chapter Five

ER

"OWWWWWWWWW!" I yelped when the young doctor who had introduced himself as Dr. Sam Heaton pressed on a few points around my wrist.

"OWWWWWW!" he yelped back as my foot shot out in response to his prodding and kicked him in the shin.

"Oops, sorry," I said.

"Th-th-that's okay," Dr. Sam stuttered, but his eyes watered and he maneuvered himself out of the way of my feet. He hardly looked old enough to be a doctor; in fact, he looked more like he belonged in the 12th grade, with his pleasant face, tousled brown hair, and pink cheeks.

"It hurt when you pressed," I said.

"Is it broken?" asked Mom.

"I can't tell until it's been x-rayed. You hang on here, and I'll go and get that organized. In the meantime, I'll get one of the nurses to give you a painkiller," said Dr. Sam, then I heard him mutter under his breath, "Might even take one myself."

"How long will it take?" I asked. "I want to go home."

We'd been in the emergency waiting room for more than three hours waiting to be seen. My wrist and my ankle were throbbing, I was hungry, and I had a headache starting.

"Not long," he said, "but it's always busy here on weekends."

As he made his way out of the small cubicle, a teenage boy with red hair who was coming the other way suddenly lurched and then vomited all over Dr. Sam's white coat.

"Eww! Gross!" I cried and then clapped my hand over my mouth because I realized I'd said it so loud that everyone in the waiting room must have heard. Behind the desk, a man who was taking the names of newcomers chuckled. I figured I'd voiced what a lot of the people who work there must think daily. "Remind me never to be a doctor," I said to Mom.

"But thank God some people choose to be," she replied, looking coyly in Dr. Sam's direction, which almost made me say "Gross!" again. I mean, eww, my mom acting like a teenage girl.

I watched Dr. Sam retreat through the doors at the end of the corridor. "I wonder if this is a typical day for him. Kicked and then someone throws up on you. What a job!"

After another hour of waiting and playing a word game with Mom to pass the time, I was taken to the x-ray unit. By then, the pill that a nurse had given me had taken effect; my wrist wasn't quite as painful, and all I felt was that I'd like to slide under one of the chairs or beds and take a nap. Once I'd been x-rayed, they saw that my ankle wasn't broken, so a nurse bandaged it up, and I was taken back to the waiting room. We had to wait to see what was wrong with my wrist.

Being sick has to be the most boring thing ever, I thought, as Mom fussed over me before going off to get us some sandwiches and a drink from the store near the hospital's main lobby. I looked around for something to do, but I couldn't see anything. I sat back in my chair and looked up at the ceiling. It was covered with white tiles, and there was a crack in the one closest to the light bulb. I glanced back down and around. A few people were sitting on the orange plastic chairs in the waiting room—an old lady in her nightgown, a fraught-looking mother with a chubby-cheeked toddler, a red-faced man who smelled of beer and had a cut on his forehead. Across from me were the cubicles where the doctors saw the patients. Most of them had the curtains pulled shut. I looked across the unit and out the window but couldn't see much from where I was. I was about to get my phone out when I saw a poster above a radiator that said the use of cell phones was NOT allowed. Seeing the sign reminded me of my new zodiac cell phone. *That's what I can do*, I thought. I can see how it works. I felt in my pocket for the phone, but couldn't find it. I stood up and had another feel around. No, it definitely wasn't there. *Did I put it somewhere?* I wondered. No. No. I definitely had it in my pocket just before the cat jumped in front of me. Bug bottoms. It must have slipped out when I fell. *Grrr.* This day really is turning out to be a major bummer.

I got up and hobbled to the reception desk and waited for what seemed like an eternity for the lady there to look at me.

Finally, she glanced up and made eye contact. "What?" she asked.

"Do you have any magazines or books or anything? I'm bored."

"Does this look like a library? No, we don't have any magazines. Where's your mother?"

"She's gone to the store."

"Then maybe she'll get you a magazine."

Her glare communicated that I was to go back to my seat, sit down, and shut up. *Hmm*, I thought. *She's an angry woman.* I sat back, closed my eyes, and tried not to focus on my wrist. It was beginning to hurt again. Try to have a nice daydream, I told myself. It's what Dad always advised me to do when I was little and we were on a long journey somewhere. Imagine that you're in a beautiful place on vacation and the sea is just feet away, lapping on the shore. The sun is shining down, the birds are singing . . . My fantasy was disturbed by the sound of someone groaning, and seconds later the powerful odor of disinfectant filled my nostrils. I opened my eyes to the bright lights above. *At least I won't have to stay here overnight,* I thought. *I can't imagine that anyone ever gets any sleep.*

As I sat there, an old man came in. I couldn't help but stare at him because he seemed so out of place—I could see by his white hair and beard that he was old, but he seemed to radiate health as if he was lit up from the inside. He scanned the people in the waiting area, and then the moment he saw me he nodded to himself and began to make his way over. *He must be nearsighted,* I thought, *because I have never set eyes on him in my life.*

When he reached me, he pulled something out of his pocket and handed it over. "I think this is yours," he said. It was my zodiac phone!

"Yes. I . . . H-how did you know?" I stuttered.

The man gave me a stern look. "It is my duty to know. And you, young lady, should be more careful. To be chosen as a Zodiac Girl is a rare honor, as it is to receive one of these phones. To lose it on your very first day, well . . . it smacks of irresponsibility, if you ask me."

"That's so unfair!" I blurted. "I fell. It wasn't my fault. It must have slipped out of my pocket."

"*That's so unfair!*" mimicked the man in a baby voice.

"*Not my fault.*"

"It wasn't. And I don't talk like that."

"Major lesson in life, young lady, and that is to take responsibility for your actions and your mistakes."

I felt myself getting very angry. "No need for the lecture," I said with a pout.

He turned to go. "Well, don't lose it again. I have better things to do with my time than chase silly young girls around with things they have lost. And do I hear a word of thanks? Not likely."

"Thanks," I said. I knew that I sounded sulky, but I'd had a miserable day. He didn't understand. "Hey. Who are you, anyway?"

"Dr. Cronus. Another one of the planets. You've met Mars and Uranus already. I've come by to let you know that as an Aries, your ruling planet is Mars, so you get Mario Ares as your guardian. He's already made himself known to you, but you can expect him to be in touch again soon to help out where he can. A few of us others will also drop by from time to time to lend a helping hand." He chuckled when he said this. "Helping hand, that's exactly what you do need, isn't it?"

Oh, for goodness' sake, I thought, *he's a nutty noodle job*. Best to humor him until Mom gets back, and then we can call security. "Oh, yes. Um . . . and which planet are you?"

He gave me another one of his stern looks. "Saturn.

38

Saturn rules Capricorn. It's a very different sign from Aries. Do you know much about your sign?"

I nodded. "Yeah, a little. Good at sports. First sign of the zodiac?"

"Yes, not *yeah*. And impatient. Can't sit still. Should look before they leap. Not like Capricorns, who think before they act," he said and pointed at my wrist. "Still, this should slow down your momentum for a while." I'm sure that it wasn't my imagination—his eyes looked gleeful as he said it.

"It's nothing serious," I said. "I think it's just a sprain."

Dr. Cronus replied. "I wouldn't bet on that!"

And then he marched off.

What a strange man, I thought.

Mom came back a few moments later with two bottles of juice, a candy bar, and a bag of potato chips.

"There wasn't much left in the store," she said as she put the items on an empty chair next to us.

I pointed to the glass doors. We could see Dr. Cronus crossing the parking lot. "See that man, Mom? He's a total loon."

Mom strained to look, shook her head, and laughed. "I don't think so, dear. That's Dr. Cronus."

"You know him?"

Mom nodded. "He's the principal of a very prestigious private school just outside Osbury. He has a fantastic reputation and gets great results. I met him at the last conference that was held for school principals. I was very impressed and think I'll use some of his methods in my school. He's very strict and old-fashioned, but it works."

"He thinks he's a planet."

Mom laughed again and patted my arm. "Honestly, Marsha, you do say some funny things sometimes."

"No, really. He thinks he's Saturn. Rules Capricorn. He just told me."

It was no use. I tried telling her about Uri, too, but she just kept laughing as if I was making it all up on purpose to entertain her.

"Oh, for heaven's sake, Marsha," she said. I had been about to show her my zodiac phone, but after her reaction, I decided not to waste my time. I would investigate these planet people and the zodiac thing on my own.

"This really has to be the most boring day of my entire life," I said, after we had sat for another age with nothing else to do but watch sick people come and go.

"Are you okay? Is there anything I can get you?" asked Mom.

"I just want to go home," I said.

She put her hand over my good one and gave me a painful smile. "Me, too."

We sat there for another hour while Mom put on her

cheerful face and voice and tried to keep me entertained. I found myself nodding off to sleep while she rattled on and woke up with a jolt when I almost slipped off the chair. *What's going on?* I wondered as I heard Dr. Sam's and Mom's voices a few feet away.

"Murmur murmur, murmur murmur."

I strained to hear what they were saying. I could hear the occasional word like ulna and fracture.

"I CAN hear you," I said. "I'm not deaf."

Mom turned around. "Sorry, darling. Dr. Heaton here says it looks like a greenstick fracture."

"Sounds like some kind of plant. Is it bad?" I asked.

Dr. Sam gave me a smile. "It's an incomplete fracture where the bone bends like a green stick. We'll have to put your arm in a cast."

"*A cast?* What kind of cast?"

"A plaster-of-Paris cast from the hand to halfway between the elbow and armpit. It's free on one side of the forearm to allow swelling and enable circulation."

"How long before it gets better?" I asked as a feeling of alarm hit my stomach.

"Hmm. Fractures of the upper limb bones take around six weeks to heal—"

"*Six weeks?*"

"It can take around half of that in younger people. With a bit of luck, you'll be up and whacking a tennis ball

41

around again in four weeks."

"*Four weeks?* Bu—but I'm in the school play. I'm the Ice Queen."

Dr. Sam and Mom exchanged worried glances.

"And when's the play?" asked the doctor.

"At the end of the month. In around three weeks."

"Hmm. Depends on the part. I think we could strap you up and you'd be okay, as long as you don't move around too much," said Dr. Sam.

"I don't say anything. I dance. I'm the main dancer. The Ice Queen." I could feel my fantasy about being the star of the show and the talk of the school begin to crack and melt like an iceberg.

"*Dance?* Oh no," said Dr. Sam. "I don't think there's going to be much chance of that. Your ankle won't take so long—it will be tender for a few weeks at least—but a greenstick fracture like yours needs time to recover correctly."

I can do this, I thought. *I can fix this. I won't give up.* I sat up and made myself snap out of the sluggish feeling that had come over me since I'd taken the painkiller. "Okay. So let's do it. Sooner we get out of here, the better and the sooner I can get on with my recovery." I held out my wrist. "Do your stuff, Doc."

Dr. Sam grimaced. "I'm afraid you won't be going home today, Marsha. We need to keep you in tonight—"

"Stay here? Overnight? Noooo. You can't be serious. It's not even a complete fracture—you just said so. Mom, tell him—"

"Darling, you have to do what the doctor says. What is it you have to do, Doctor?"

"She'll go up to the ward and be put into a special kind of sling. It holds the arm in the air. This is to reduce the swelling and makes the operation easier."

"OPERATION! WARD? Whoa there a moment. What operation?"

"We need to manipulate the fracture. Don't worry, you'll be put to sleep so you won't feel it, and it means we can do the manipulation without any need for surgical incision. We use traction and rotation, and then we'll put your arm in plaster of Paris from your knuckles to just above your elbow."

A frightened voice was getting louder in the pit of my stomach. It just said one word: NooooOOOOOOOO!

"I . . . I . . . But . . ." The idea of anyone rotating, manipulating, or coming anywhere near my sore wrist made me feel faint.

"How long will it take?" asked Mom.

"The operation will take around half an hour. And it won't be too painful afterward."

"Not too painful? I . . . No. No. I don't do pain. Mom, tell him I want a second opinion."

"Don't worry, we'll give you acetaminophen," said the doctor.

"*Acetaminophen?*" I wasn't feeling reassured. I needed chocolate. I reached out with my good hand for the candy bar that Mom had bought.

"Enjoy that while you can," said Dr. Sam. "If we're going to do you first thing, you'll need to starve from midnight tonight."

"No breakfast?" I asked.

"Nope. And you won't be able to eat until after the operation," said the doctor.

I. Could. Not. Believe. It.

My fear began to change into a surge of rage as a nurse appeared with a hospital gown, and I saw the last remnants of my dream life disappear. Mom took the gown from the nurse, and I remembered the words of Dr. Cronus when I'd said that it was only a sprain. "Don't bet on it," he'd said. *Grrr to you, whoever you are*, I thought. *Grrr, grrr, grrr!* You can take your zodiac stuff, Dr. Cronus, and you can take your ugly hospital gown, Dr. Sam, and bury them in the mud. *AAAAAArrrrrgh!*

Chapter Six

Drama queens

"I'll be back in the morning," said Mom, after I was settled on my bed and the nurse had told her three times that she had to leave. Her eyes filled up with tears, and she ignored all her requests to go, even though the nurse was built like a heavyweight wrestler and Mom is a size four. A badge on the nurse's uniform told us that her name was Abbie. She was so sweet with Mom, talking to her like she was around five and like she was the one having to stay in the hospital. I felt torn. Part of me wanted her to go so that I could get the attention that I deserved, and part of me wanted her to stay because I didn't want to be alone in a strange place. The part that wanted her to go seemed to be winning. I felt annoyed with her. I was the one in pain, the one whose life had been ruined, but she was acting like it had all happened to her.

"I'm okay, Mom. You can go," I said, but I still had my sulky face on. I couldn't help it. I had never felt so miserable. I had been zooming along nicely in the fast lane, and now life had shoved a great big STOP sign on the road.

"You really have to leave now," repeated Nurse Abbie. Her dark round face looked weary as if she had had a long day.

Mom stuck out her bottom lip, and it wobbled like she was about to burst into tears. "Just another minute with my baby . . ."

"I'm not a baby. I'm twelve! Just go!" I blurted. "I'll be fine."

"Do you have any painkillers?" Mom asked the nurse.

"Oh, don't worry. We'll provide them for Marsha if she needs medication," said Nurse Abbie.

"Not for her! For me," said Mom, and the nurse gave her an exasperated look before walking away.

Mom wrapped me in an enormous hug, clinging onto me when I tried to pull away. "Mom, just go. I will be okay, at least I probably will. Um . . . tell Dad—just in case anything goes wrong with my operation tomorrow—that I didn't mind that he didn't come to the hospital and felt it was more important to go out with his football friends. He didn't know that it's as serious as it is." (*That will make him feel guilty*, I thought. *And I hope it does, too!*) "And tell Cissie that if I die, she can have my DVDs—no, no, let Lois have them. And Eleanor can have my pink baseball cap, the one with 'Princess' written on it. She's always wanted that."

"Oh, don't talk like that. You know your dad would have been here," Mom said through sniffles. "I told him you'd just had a fall—I mean, it's not the first time, is it? But it's never meant an operation before. Oh, oh, I can't leave you like this."

"Yes. Yes, you can. Go on, back home, to my sisters, to your comfy bed. Oh, I do hope I see them again . . . yes, go . . . I'll be all right in this cold, strange place. I'll be fine."

I put on my best heroic face at this point, but it only made Mom look more anxious.

"Oh, come on, Mom. It's not like I'm really going to die or anything, although . . . I have heard of people going into the hospital and never coming out again."

Mom let out an audible gasp, and I saw the girl in the bed to the left glance over. She looked like she was about to burst out laughing. She was around my age and looked like an African princess lying propped up on pillows—pillows that didn't look like the lumpy hospital kind on my bed, and she was dressed in bright-red silk PJs that most definitely weren't hospital issue. There appeared to be something wrong with her leg, because it was propped up by pillows under the blanket. I suddenly felt embarrassed for Mom getting so carried away. She could be such a drama queen!

"My darling baby," she murmured into my hair. "Your poor arm and your poor hair, too."

"Mo-om," I groaned.

"Mrs. Leibowitz!" called Nurse Abbie.

"Coming, coming, going, going!" Mom called back, and she finally let me go. She got up, sighed loudly à la tragic heroine, with the back of her hand on her forehead, and made her way down the room. At the end she stopped, turned, sighed again, and flounced through the double doors, leaving them swinging in her wake.

I glanced over at the girl in the red PJs. She was staring at me.

"Nice performance," she said.

I rolled my eyes up to the ceiling. "I know. She's always like that," I said. "So embarrassing."

"Not her," said the girl. "You."

"What do you mean? Me?"

The girl laughed. "All that, 'Oh, I might die' stuff, laying it on with a shovel."

I felt outraged. "*Laying it on with a shovel?* Um, excuse me, but you don't even know what happened to me."

The girl shrugged. "Yeah, I do. You broke or twisted your arm or something. I heard the nurses talking about it before you came up. Your poor mom. You were really making her suffer."

"I-I—" I was lost for words. Didn't she have eyes as well as ears? Couldn't she see my terrible dilemma? "It's not just this, you know. I was up to play the main part in

48

the school play. All that's gone now, I bet. My whole life is ruined because of this . . ." I turned away. I didn't want to talk to her anymore. She was obviously so wrapped up in herself that she didn't care about anyone else.

"You're not the only one whose life isn't working out. So get over it. At least you will. You'll recover. There are people in here who are really sick, you know."

I turned back to look at her. "Oh, sorry. I . . . um . . . are you very sick?"

"Not me. I'll recover, too," she said and then lowered her voice and jerked her chin toward someone in the third bed in our section. "Amy, down there."

I couldn't see much of who was in that bed, just the top of someone's head, someone with brown hair. *Oh God, there are sick people in here*, I thought.

"What's the matter with her?" I whispered back to the girl, but she had turned back to her magazine as if she had lost interest in me. "Hey, you," I hissed.

The girl turned around. "Skye," she said. "My name is Skye, not hey, you. You need to learn some manners."

"I . . ." I felt like someone had poured a bucket of cold water over me. *I don't like you*, I thought. "And you need to learn to be more sensitive," I said. "This is my first time in the hospital, you know, and although, okay, I might not be dying, I don't like it, and I don't want to be here."

Skye shrugged. "Welcome to my world," she said,

before returning to her magazine. I decided not to ask what was wrong with Amy. In fact, I wouldn't talk to Skye at all if I could help it. Just because we were in the same room didn't mean that we had to be friends.

I looked around at my surroundings. I hadn't had a chance when we'd first gotten up here because Dr. Sam had been waiting for me and had swished the curtain around my bed while he hoisted my arm up into the air in the weird sling thing. I felt ridiculous when he'd finished. I would have to sit upright all night with my arm bound up in sky-blue spongy stuff, and the whole contraption was strung up to a hook on the wall beside the bed.

"For your comfort," he had said, but I couldn't get my head around that. Surely it would be way more comfy if I could lie down with my hand by my side? It felt cumbersome having it up in the air because I couldn't move it. *This is how prisoners who are being tortured must feel*, I thought, as I squirmed to get into a position that was comfortable. Only I haven't done anything bad.

From my vantage point, the ward appeared to be divided up into different sections. There were four beds in my part, one of which was empty. I glanced down to Amy's bed, but I still couldn't see her, and at that moment a female doctor walked past and pulled the curtains around her. I looked around at the rest of the room. The walls were white, the curtains a bright turquoise, and the lights overhead were really bright. I didn't like what was happening, and I didn't want to be there. I wanted to be at home under my soft, cozy pink comforter, surrounded by my things. A wave of anxiety came over me when I thought of what I was in for in the next few days. I had slept away from home before, loads of times, at camp or sleepovers, but never in a place like this. A place that was full of strangers and sharp steel instruments and the smell of disinfectant. Suddenly, I wanted Mom back. *It's only for a night,* I told myself. *You can do this.* I blinked back sudden tears and hoped that no one had seen and thought that I was a wimp.

"Hey, newbie!" called the African princess. "What's your name?"

"Marsha," I said, but I didn't look at her when I said it, and I hoped she got the message that I didn't want to talk to her.

The noise of a cart being wheeled into our room disturbed any conversation, and the smell of boiled meat hit my nostrils.

"Dinner," said Nurse Abbie. She bustled over to me, pushed a movable table over the bed, and then plopped down a tray of food. A piece of meat with onions and some canned corn. It looked and smelled disgusting.

"No, thanks," I said.

"Aren't you hungry?"

"Yes, but I'm not eating that."

Nurse Abbie laughed. "Can't say I blame you, darlin', but it's all you's a-gettin'."

"Then I won't eat anything."

"I'll leave it here a while," said the nurse. "You might change your mind later when you get hungry."

She moved off toward Skye. I felt so frustrated. The smell of the food was making me feel nauseated, but there was nothing I could do. I couldn't push it away, nor could I get up and walk away.

"Need some help?" asked Skye.

I made a face at the food. "This smells disgusting," I said.

Skye laughed. "You're quite the princess, aren't you?"

"No," I said. I objected to her insinuating that I was a princess, as if I was spoiled or something, even though I had thought that she was a princess, too. "It's just that it smells horrible."

"This isn't the Hilton, you know," said Skye. "So, unless you've got something tucked away, Abbie was right—that's all you're going to get."

I shrugged and pushed the food away with my good hand. I must have overestimated the edge of the movable table, because the plate slipped and clattered onto the floor, causing Nurse Abbie to jump.

"Oh, for heaven's sake," said Skye. "She's having a

tantrum now."

"No. I . . ." I wasn't having a tantrum. *She* so *doesn't get me*, I thought, as Abbie came over and, letting out a weary sigh, began to pick up the mess. "I'm sorry. I didn't mean to do that." I felt tears prick the back of my eyes. I wanted my mom and my dad and Cissie and Eleanor and Lois. People who were on my side. An overwhelming feeling of frustration overtook me, and I felt worried that I might start blubbing. I *so* didn't want to do that in case Skye saw and laughed again. She had clearly formed a bad opinion of me, plus there was something about her that seemed very cool, and I didn't want her to think that I was uncool, a big baby, scared of being away from home.

The curtains around the third bed were pulled back, and the nurse and doctor who had been in there came out. Their expressions were serious. I glanced over to try to see Amy but couldn't see much—still just a head with brown hair on the pillow. I wondered what her story was. I thought about asking Skye, but I noticed that she had put on her headphones.

After a while, Nurse Abbie came and took away the food with another weary sigh. I thought about asking her about Amy, but by the way she brusquely cleared everything away, I gauged that she wasn't in the mood for talking. She positioned the small TV that was attached to the ceiling so that I could see it, and she handed me the remote. After she left, I flicked through channels, but there wasn't much on. In the end I watched a detective show just to pass the time.

At around 10:00 P.M., the lights went out. I heard Skye snuggle down, but Amy hadn't stirred at all.

"Night, newbie," whispered Skye.

"My name's Marsha," I whispered back.

"Night, newbie," Skye whispered again. I didn't respond, and after a while I could tell by her even breathing that she had fallen asleep.

Lucky thing, I thought. It was so weird sitting in my strange bed in the dark. I couldn't even lie down, put the covers over my head, and pretend that I wasn't there. In my upright position, my eyes grew accustomed to the dark, and the room filled with shadows. Outside I could hear the drone of distant traffic. Inside all was quiet aside from the occasional sounds of footsteps, voices, and a door opening or closing in the distance. I knew that I was in a hospital surrounded by people—doctors, nurses, and patients—but I had never felt so alone in my entire life.

Chapter Seven

Op day one

"Wargh!" I cried as I felt a presence next to me. I opened my eyes. I didn't know where I was. My eyes adjusted to the soft light of morning. It wasn't a dream. It was a living nightmare. Bright overhead lights came on, flooding light into every shadow, and I realized that I was still in the hospital.

My brain hurt. My arm hurt. My eyes hurt. And I needed to go to the bathroom.

"Just checking that you're okay there," said a small blond nurse. I looked at her badge. It said that her name was Cheryl.

"I-I need to move. My arm feels numb, and I need to go to the bathroom."

"I'll unhook you, and you can go," said the nurse.

It had been a horrible night. The whole time I could hear the nurses talking and laughing in the nurses' station down the corridor at the end of the ward, and there were so many disturbances: lights going on and off, someone being brought in on a gurney, lowered voices, strange beeps, moans, the sound of water dripping, machines clicking, and someone (I suspected Skye) snoring. The thought of my lovely snuggly bed in my quiet room made me ache with homesickness. At last, however, I must have fallen into a light doze in the early hours because I wasn't aware of anything more until Cheryl had appeared.

"Won't be long now," said Cheryl again. "They'll come and get you soon."

Great, I thought, *the sooner the better, then I'm out of here.* "Soon when?"

"Maybe in around an hour."

"*An hour?* " It sounded like such a long time.

Cheryl nodded and shoved some type of contraption in my ear. It made me jump.

"What's that?"

"It takes your temperature," she said, and then she put a black plastic armband around my arm. I knew from yesterday that it took my blood pressure.

"Can I have a hot chocolate or some juice?" I asked when she'd finished.

Cheryl shook her head. "Nothing until after the op."

"So why did you wake me?"

"To check that you were all right."

I groaned. "I *was* all right. I was asleep. And now I'm not. So I'm not all right. Why didn't you just leave me?"

"It's my job to check on people in the morning."

"That's so totally cruel. Surely the kindest thing would be to let people sleep."

Cheryl shrugged. "Rules are rules." She unhooked me so that I could go to the bathroom, and then she tottered off to poke Skye awake. She didn't seem too pleased about it, either, and groaned loudly. "Leave me alone."

I hobbled to the bathroom. My ankle was still sore, but not as bad as yesterday. When I came back into my section, I saw Cheryl tiptoe over to Amy's bed and take her temperature. She didn't wake up. *Lucky thing*, I thought. *She's dead to the world.* And then I shuddered. *She was lying very still. Ohmigod, maybe she* is *dead!*

Skye had turned over and gone back to sleep. Cheryl hooked my arm up again, but I couldn't get back to sleep. I was wide awake. I saw that there was a remote control by the side of the bed that was labeled "bed adjuster." I decided to press a few of the buttons to see if it would make my bed more comfortable. I pressed on the controls with my good hand to see what it did. Legs up, legs down. *Cool*, I thought. Mattress up a bit, down a bit. Up, down, forward, back. And then my hand slipped, and the bottom half of my bed began to rise. My legs went up and up— if I wasn't careful, I was going to fold in half.

"Oooooo whoaaaa, Nurse!" I cried.

Cheryl was there in an instant, and I could see that she

was having a hard time not laughing.

"It's not funny," I said. I felt close to tears again. "How long before they come to get me?"

Cheryl checked her watch. "Forty-five minutes or so," she said, and she scurried off back down the ward.

I groaned again.

"Be quiet, newbie!" Skye called from her bed. "Some of us are trying to get some sleep here."

"And some of us are trying to find something to do. It's so boring in here," I said and kicked off the sheets. "And so hot."

In reply, Skye put a pillow over her head. Soon afterward, she got out of bed and hobbled out of the room with her toiletries bag, so I presumed that she was going to the bathroom.

While she was gone, Cheryl came over and said that my cell phone had bleeped. Someone had been trying to get through.

"My mom," I said.

"No. He said he was your guardian."

Must be Dad, I thought, *and about time*. "But I thought that we couldn't use our cell phones in here."

"You can send text messages and occasionally take a call," said Cheryl. "Do you want me to get it for you?"

I nodded, and Cheryl rooted around in my drawer. She pulled out the zodiac phone and was about to hand it to me.

"Not that one. The silver one," I said. "I won that one. I don't even know if it works."

Cheryl looked back in the drawer and then handed me both phones. "Yes, it does. It was this red phone that was bleeping, but you can see if you have any messages on both."

I looked on the screen of my usual phone. There was one message, but it wasn't from Dad. It was a text from Lois.

Ohmigod. Wl cm 2 C U 6pm. Lois. XXXXX.

I checked again to see if I had missed the one from Dad, but there was definitely nothing else on there. I looked on my zodiac phone. I pressed what seemed like the ON button on the keypad, and seconds later, it bleeped that I had a message. I found the message section and read:

Zodiac Girl. Yours is the sign of the warrior. You are ruled by Mars, god of war. My message to you is be brave. Keep fighting. I will be in touch. Your guardian, Mario Ares, a.k.a. Mars.

Wow, I thought. *That's kind of strange. How could he have known what happened to me? Maybe he didn't. Not really. Maybe it's a random message that they send out to all Aries girls? Yeah. I guess that's it. You could tell anyone to keep fighting, and it would probably apply to their situation. Whatever. It's still a cool phone.*

As I played around with the buttons, I noticed that there were already ten numbers in the address book. I scrolled down.

Mr. O.: the Sun

Selene: the Moon

Hermie: Mercury

Nessa: Venus

P. J.: Pluto

Joe: Jupiter

Mario: Mars

Captain John Dory: Neptune

Dr. Cronus: Saturn. That batty old man from the waiting room, I realized.

Uri: Uranus. *Uri Uranus?* I asked myself. Wasn't he the man on the unicycle who waited with me after I'd fallen? His name was Uri, wasn't it? Hmm. Weird.

As I was wondering about the names, a young black man with dreadlocks, wearing green coveralls, came through the double doors with what looked like the breakfast cart. He went from section to section, and when he got to ours, Amy was still asleep, but Skye sat up and chose Shredded Wheat and toast.

"Only things they can't ruin," she said and started eating moments later.

"What are you in for?" I asked.

Skye shrugged. "They found an alien living in my stomach."

I laughed.

She didn't. Her expression was deadly serious.

"Oh . . . I . . ." I had a momentary panic that maybe it was some type of rare disease, but then she pointed at her right foot under the sheets. With effort, she poked it out from under the covers, and I could see that it was in a cast.

"Duh. My ankle," she said. She turned back to her cereal as if to say that was the end of that conversation.

After breakfast, the nurses seemed to go into overdrive. I couldn't see much from where I was, but I could hear the activity. All that time, there wasn't a peep out of Amy in the third bed.

"Is that girl all right?" I asked Cheryl as she approached my bed with a bald male nurse in green scrubs.

Cheryl breathed out heavily. "Not sure. Oh, and here's Jacob to wheel you down."

Jacob gave me a friendly smile, and all further questions about Amy went out the window as I thought, *At last. Now, I can get this thing over with and get out of here.* I sat up, and even though I wasn't looking forward to what they were going to do, I put on my best brave face. "I'm ready," I said. "Do your worst."

Jacob smiled again. "I am sorry," he said. "But we have had a number of emergencies. An accident out on the expressway—a pileup—and there have been several cases brought in that were urgent."

"Um, well, thanks for the news flash, but what does that have to do with me?"

"We'll have to delay your op until tomorrow," he said.

"Delay? Nooo, but . . . I've been waiting all night."

"I know, and we're sorry, but in these cases, we have to prioritize," he said and began to back out of the ward. "Got to run."

"Noooooo. But . . . what about MEEEEEEE?" I called after him.

Nurse Cheryl smiled. "Well, at least you can have a hot chocolate. Should I bring you a mug and some toast?"

"No. I'll go home and wait there," I said.

"I don't think the doctors will let that happen," said Cheryl. "Oh no, not likely." She bustled off down the ward.

I felt like throwing something at someone. Normally, I am not a tantrum sort of person, but I felt indignant. Didn't anyone realize that I had spent the whole night sitting up, starving, and uncomfortable? This. Couldn't. Be. Happening.

"I DON'T WANT ANYTHING!" I shouted, causing Skye to glance over and raise an eyebrow. "And you can stop staring at me." She shrugged her shoulders as if to say, whatever.

It *so* wasn't fair. If I'd felt miserable last night when I'd come in, it was nothing compared with how I felt now. Another day in this brightly lit dump? I couldn't bear it. "CHERYL!"

She turned back. "What is it now?"

"I am so uncomfortable. Can't you unhook me for a while, please? I can't bear sitting here like this."

"I can put you in a high arm sling for a while if you would like, but only for a while, because that special sling helps reduce the swelling. And don't shout like that. You'll scare the other patients."

I don't care, I thought, but when I glanced over at Amy's bed, I saw that she had woken up and was looking around like a startled mouse, and then I did feel a little mean. At least I'll be getting out of here soon; she looks like she's in for a long while. She looked over at me, and I gave her a little wave with my good hand and smiled. She looked like she could do with a friend.

After a short while, Cheryl brought me some breakfast—white toast and jelly.

"I don't eat white bread," I said. "Don't you have any whole-wheat bread?"

Cheryl laughed. "Ah, you're quite something," she said, and she left the plate of toast on the table that could be moved across the bed.

I maneuvered myself as best as I could in order to eat it, and actually, it wasn't too bad. Skye was right. It would be hard to ruin toast, and the mug of hot chocolate was wonderful after not being able to drink for so long.

After breakfast, I watched people come and go. Dad called at around 7:30 A.M., and I filled him in on what had happened.

"Oh," he said. "Your mother called the hospital first thing, and they said you were first on the list to go down to the operating room."

"Change of plans. There was an accident, and now I'm last on the list. Dad, can't you do something about this? Get me into another hospital? Surely you know someone who knows someone. I'm in agony. Or at least get me out of here for today. There's no point in staying here like this."

"I'll come in later with your mother," said Dad. "Sit tight, and I'll see what I can do."

"Don't be long. It's like time has slowed down in here."

After Dad's call, I had another look at the zodiac phone. As I was playing with it, it bleeped that I had another text message.

```
Give   me   a   call   when   you   need   some
entertaining. Uri
```

That would be nice, I thought, *he seemed like a kind man, even if he was a little eccentric. Some entertainment would be great.*

I decided to type a message and send it to all of the names in the address book and see what happened. There was nothing else to do, it would pass the time, and I had nothing to lose.

I wrote my message.

```
Zodiac Girl in need of help. In the hospital.
Need   supplies,   entertainment,   pampering.
Urgent. SOS.
```

Then I pressed SEND TO ALL. *Okay,* I said to myself, *let's see if this zodiac thing really is a prize worth having!*

As I put the phone back in the drawer next to the bed, I noticed Skye watching me. "What do you have there?" she asked.

"Just a cell phone," I said. "I won it on the Internet. It's supposed to be a zodiac phone, but I'm not really sure what it does yet."

She got out of her bed, hobbled over, and sat on the edge of mine. I gave her the phone to look at.

"It's a cool phone," she said as she turned it over. "Stylish."

"Thanks," I said. I was about to ask her more about her leg when the staff nurse came over and asked Skye to go back to her bed so that her doctor could see her. Minutes later, the double doors at the end of the room opened, and the doctor appeared. He went to Skye's bed and swished the curtains closed. I did my best to hear what he was saying, but I couldn't catch many words.

After he left, Skye seemed subdued. When I glanced over, she was lying with her eyes open, looking up at the ceiling. I glanced farther along the room. Amy was also awake. She, too, was lying on her back, staring at the ceiling. If I'd been able to move, I might have gotten out of my bed and gone to talk to her, but I was still fastened to the wall with my spongy blue handcuff, and I didn't want to do any more damage to my arm by unhooking it myself. *Ah, happy days, NOT*, I thought, as I glanced at my watch. It was only 8:00 A.M. I looked up at the ceiling to see what was so fascinating to the others up there.

Big white ceiling tiles.

A long fluorescent light tube.

A bit of pink balloon material in the far right of the ceiling. I wonder how that got up there.

I looked around the room.

And back up at the ceiling.

And back around the room.

I looked at my watch. It was 8:10 A.M.

Bug bottoms. I AM SO BORED, I thought. It's like time has stopped. In all my life, I don't think I have sat still for so long. Aaargh. No. No. Okay, I can do this. I'm an Aries, and as Mario said, we are fighters. I'm not a giver-in. I've never admitted defeat about anything in my life. I just have to get the right attitude. Yogis and guru-type people do it when they meditate in remote caves in India. I've seen them on TV. They don't have anything to distract them. No radio, no movies, no nothing. And they find peace. Maybe I'll come out of here totally enlightened. Maybe I'll just float out of here. Saint Marsha. Swami Marsha. That will be me. Oh . . . I wish that there was something to do. I don't think Skye looks like she wants to talk right now. And Amy, she looks really sick. I wonder if it's contagious. Oh God, I hope not. Poor thing. When I can move, I'll try to cheer her up. I wonder if she feels lonely in here, too. It's weird being away from home and not knowing what's going to happen. Oh, it's SO boring here. I'll see if I can catch the nurse's attention. She keeps walking past, always in a hurry, never makes eye contact. Oh God, I wish something would happen. So much for being a Zodiac Girl. Since I got that news, everything has gone wrong. And nothing's happened since I sent out my cry for help to the zodiac people.

An hour later, and still no one had come.

Another hour, and still no one.

Just nurses, cleaners, the occasional doctor, a lady with

a beverage cart. No exciting zodiac people, that was for sure.

At last it was visiting hour, and I waited in anticipation for the nurses to open the doors. Mom was the first through, and she came bustling in, laden down with promising-looking bags. I had never been so glad to see her in all my life, not even after the summer camp when I was nine and it had rained nonstop and everyone had gotten a stomach bug and been utterly miserable. Mom had brought lots of goodies and a card that Lois had dropped by that morning. In the bags were magazines, fruit, chocolate, a toiletries bag, my sky-blue pajamas, and a few books.

"I've had an awful night," she said (like I hadn't), "but I've come through it and decided that I have to be brave. Be positive."

"Good for you," I said sarcastically, but she didn't seem to get it.

"Yes, isn't it?" she replied. "I have to be strong. For you, dear."

"Where's Dad?"

"Parking the car," she replied, and, indeed, he did appear around five minutes later. I felt a lump in my throat seeing his familiar round face, and when he gave me a hug, I breathed in his safe "Dad" smell of lemon aftershave mixed with pencil shavings. He was dressed in his weekend casuals of jeans and a fleece, and his dark hair, which was usually neatly combed back for the office on weekdays, flopped over his forehead.

"You have to get me out of here," I said. "Anything you can do about another hospital?"

Dad chuckled. "I've had a word with the doctor, and you're in the best possible hands here. Chin up. Be my brave girl."

Chin up? Brave girl? He clearly had no idea. I decided not to speak to him for the rest of the visit. Not that he noticed. He ate my grapes and read my magazine like it was enough that he'd simply shown up. I could not believe it. And Mom was blabbering about what was on TV, what was in the paper, what and who she'd seen on the way up to the ward. What had happened to the tearful Mom of last night? She really did seem to have had a personality change and was being brusque and breezy. It was very annoying.

Luckily, the things she left were enough to pass the time until the second visiting hour in the early evening, and this time Lois came back with her. She, too, had brought me presents. A magazine and the loan of her fluffy pink pig toy (which was sweet because I knew that she had slept with him since she was three years old, so it was a big thing for her to let him go for a night). I was touched by that, I really was, but I also felt annoyed with her. And

Mom. They both put on drippy faces, like they were so sorry for me, and talked to me like I had lost my brain.

"There will be other plays," said Lois, and she patted my good hand.

I pulled back my hand. "No, there won't," I replied. "Not other shows with Ollie—"

"Swoon, swoon," said Lois.

I rolled my eyes. I didn't feel like saying "swoon, swoon" like we always did. "As I was saying, not with Ollie or his dad. It was my one big chance."

"There will be other opportunities," said Mom in a sugary voice. "You're still young."

Lois nodded. "You're still young. You've got your whole life ahead of you."

"No! You don't understand," I said. I couldn't believe that Lois was coming out with the same garbage as Mom. If anyone should have understood, it was her, but she clearly didn't. I saw Skye glance over. She had an amused look in her eyes. I stuck out my tongue at her. I felt angry. Angry with everyone. I couldn't help it and even though there was a part of me that was telling myself not to be a bratty princess, I couldn't pull myself out of it. It felt like I had quicksand around me, and I was being sucked down into it.

I glanced over at Skye again. She had a lot of visitors around her bed. I did a quick count. Six. Two big ladies, two middle-aged men who were probably their husbands, and a boy and girl who looked like they were in their 20s. Relatives, by the looks of them, and they were having a merry old time, gossiping and eating the food that they'd brought in. *It must be something all visitors do*, I thought, as I watched Lois pop another one of my grapes into her mouth. Amy had only one visitor, a tall pale lady who looked like her mom. They were very quiet and sat in silence, holding hands and watching the rest of us for most of the hour. There was something about Amy that looked so sad; my heart went out to her.

When the evening visiting time was over and all the visitors had left apart from mine, I felt so envious of Mom and Lois being able to get up and walk out.

"Please don't leave me here," I begged, and I put on my best I-am-in-agony face. "Please. I hate it in here. You don't know how awful it is and how much pain I'm in." I let out a groan and a sob. *If that doesn't get me out of here, I don't know what will*, I thought, as Lois looked at me anxiously. "Ooo, oooo, ahhhh, ooch, ooch."

Sadly, Mom really did seem to have had a personality change since last night, like someone had flipped a switch in her and she had gone into her "we must be strong" persona. "Darling, it's only for one more night," she said, and then she went into a cutesy, little-girl voice. "Be my big gwown-up girl and show us all how bwave you can be."

"It's all right for you," I said. "And you, Lois. You can go back to your homes, with fridges full of food and beds with comfy pillows, while I have to stay here and suffer."

This time, Skye did laugh, and out loud, too.

"And you can shut up!" I called across to her.

Mom looked shocked. "Marsha. That's not like you. You must be nice to the other girls in here." She turned to Skye. "I must apologize for my daughter. She's not herself."

Skye gave Mom a winning smile. "No probs. It can be hard for the younger ones being away from their moms and dads."

"Thank you, dear," said Mom and turned back to me. "What a charming girl."

Behind Mom, Skye stuck out her tongue at me.

I hate you, I thought, as Mom and Lois walked toward the double doors and the exit and freedom. *I hate everyone.*

To my left, Skye chuckled softly.

I wanted to kill her.

Chapter Eight

Op day two

Oh, noooooo! I thought when I awoke the following day to find that I was still in the ward. I had been dreaming that I was at home in my own bed. Nurse Cheryl took my blood pressure and my temperature, and the bright ceiling lights came on, flooding the ward with unnatural light. *This is like that movie* Groundhog Day, *where the main character keeps reliving the same day*, I thought, as I watched the ward staff go into the same routines as yesterday and patients begin to stir in their beds.

Luckily, I didn't have to wait long this time before Jacob arrived in his green scrubs. "First on the list today, Marsha," he said. "It will all be over before you know it. Ready for a little ride?"

I gave him a weak smile back and tried not to let the feeling of fear overtake me as the nurses got me ready. *It will be okay*, I told myself. *I'm glad it's happening at last because the sooner we do it, the sooner I'll be out of here and back where I belong.*

Fifteen minutes later, I was on a gurney being wheeled

through brightly-lit corridors. Part of me felt like sitting up, leaping off the gurney, and making a run for it, but another, more sensible part knew that there was no getting out of it. Once in the anesthetist's room, a big smiley man, also in green hospital scrubs, fussed around. Dr. Sam made a brief appearance and touched my foot as if to say, don't worry, I'm here, but I wasn't reassured. The urge to get up and make a run for it was still there. *Too late*, I realized as the big smiley man came at me with a needle.

"This won't hurt," he said as he put it in my arm. "You'll have a sensation of cold and then you'll go to sleep, and it will all be over."

I felt the prick of the needle and waited for the sensation. *I can't feel the cold*, I thought. *It's not working. It's NOT WORKING! I'm going to be awake all the way through the operation. Oh, no . . . oooo. Zzzzzzzzzzzzzzzzzzzzzzzzzzzzzzzzzzzzzzzzzzzzzzzzz* . . .

I awoke some time later. I was back in the room. It was all over, and Mom was next to my bed and my arm was in a sling tucked down by my side. After a slight hiccup (I felt groggy when I came around and threw up all over Mom!), I was allowed a glass of juice and some toast, and not long after that I began to feel a little nauseated but almost back to normal.

"How does the wrist feel?" Mom asked.

I focused on the area where it had been fractured. "Better, actually. It's still a little sore, but it feels okay, and at least I don't have to sit upright anymore. I can't tell you how heavenly it feels to be able to lie down! When do I get out?"

"Soon," said Mom. "I think the nurse said that Dr. Heaton wanted to do another x-ray and check in on you afterward, and then you can probably go home later today."

"Phew. Nightmare almost over," I said. "What time exactly?"

"Around three, he said."

After yesterday's visitors, the ward seemed quiet. I got up and found the bathroom and clumsily brushed my teeth with my good hand. "Soon I'll be free," I said to my reflection. I did look odd. Being away from mirrors, I'd forgotten that my hair was white, plus now that the gel had worn off, I could see that the bleach had made it very dry. And it itched. Mom had tied it back neatly for me when she'd been in, but I was longing to give it a good wash. "You've got hair like straw, my dear," I said to myself in the mirror.

When I went back to bed, I looked at the clock. Eleven. *Four more hours*, I thought. I did my best to keep myself occupied with my books and magazines, but I was grateful when a nurse came to take me for the x-ray, since that made the time go even faster.

When I got back to the room, Skye was reading and Amy was sleeping, but they were no longer my concern. In a few hours they, along with this room, would be history.

One o'clock came around. 1:05. 1:10. 1:15. I read a little. *One hour and 45 minutes to go*, I told myself. *Can't wait. Can't wait.* I watched TV for a while, but when I looked at the clock again, it seemed like only seconds had gone by. *Time in the hospital really does go slower than anywhere else on the planet*, I thought, looking at the clock again. 1:40.

When Dr. Sam came to check on me, I was sitting up trying to look as well as I could, and I had my regular cell phone ready to call Mom to let her know that she could come to get me. *Please, please, please let me go home this afternoon*, I thought, as he approached the bed.

He asked me a few questions about my wrist and how I felt.

"Great. I feel great. Thanks for everything. Now can I go home?"

Dr. Sam grimaced. "Didn't the nurse tell you?"

My stomach tightened into a knot. "Tell me what?"

"About the x-ray machine?"

"No. Why? What? Is there something still wrong with my wrist?"

"No. No, nothing like that," said Dr. Sam. "It's just that

we're having problems with the x-ray machine, and we couldn't get a clear picture."

"But don't you have other machines?"

Dr. Sam nodded. "We do, but they're all busy. The lines have been waiting here for hours. People wait for months for their appointments."

"So when can I do it again?"

"Hopefully in the morning. The technicians are looking at it now, but even if it gets fixed today, we have to wait our turn for it, and the emergency cases always take precedence. You shouldn't have to be here too long. You'll just have to stay in another night."

"Wha—? Another night? Again? No. Please. Can't I go home and then come back tomorrow?"

Dr. Sam shook his head. "With your type of injury, there's a slight risk of swelling. We need to keep you where we can keep an eye on it until we're one hundred percent certain."

"But—"

"Be a couple of days tops. It's for your own good."

"*Couple of days?* You just said one more night." The nightmare was getting worse and worse.

Dr. Sam shrugged. "You can never be too sure. I hope it will be tomorrow, but it depends on what the problem with the machine is."

I could feel something in the pit of my stomach, like

a churning volcano, burning, burning, ERUPTING into a noise in my throat. "NOOOOOOOO. Please. Let me go home, please."

Dr. Sam shook his head. "Come on, now. It's not that bad," he said. Then his pager went off, and he began to move toward the doors, giving me a cheery wave as he went.

I. Could. Not. Believe. It!

"This *so* isn't fair!" I called after him.

But he was gone, and so were my hopes of freedom.

Chapter Nine

Mr. Mars

Two o'clock.

Three-o'clock.

Three-fifteen.

Three-twenty.

Three-twenty-five.

What was going on with the clock? Surely time couldn't be going so slowly?

At 4:00 P.M., Mom arrived for the afternoon visiting hour, and I saw the nurses explain the situation to her.

"Oh, darling, I am sorry. I did call, and they told me, which is why I didn't come earlier," she said when she came over to my bed. "But it won't be long. Only another day or so."

"*Another day or so?* You just don't understand. Something has happened to time in here," I said. "It has slowed down. It's like being stuck in a time warp that never moves on."

A flicker of a smile crossed Mom's face.

"What?" I asked. "What's funny?"

"Nothing, darling, just . . . it was the way you put that. It was cute. *Stuck in a time warp.*"

I didn't feel cute. I decided that it was her fault. All of it. The fall. The x-ray machine. All of it. And I wasn't going to speak to her, other than asking two questions.

"Is Lois coming in later?"

Mom shook her head. "She has a rehearsal for the school play."

My stomach sank. I felt so jealous. I would have been doing my own rehearsals tomorrow night. With Ollie. The thought of it all happening without me made me feel like crying.

"What about Cissie and Eleanor? Are either of them coming in?"

"No, darling. They thought you'd be out tonight and that they would see you at home."

"Oh, did they? Well, you can go now. Seeing as none of you appear to really care, you may as well stop this pretense."

Mom put her hand on my bandaged wrist. "Ow!" I said and winced. It didn't actually hurt, but I wanted her to suffer, too.

"Oh, Marsha, I am sorry. Does it hurt a lot?"

I glanced over at Skye to make sure that she wasn't watching me with her amused look, but she was busy with her own visitor, one of the ladies from Sunday who I figured was her mom. I nodded. "It hurts more than you will ever know," I said, and I stuck out my bottom lip. At the back of my mind, I could hear an inner voice say, *You are acting like such a precious princess, Marsha Leibowitz. Get over yourself.* But I couldn't help it. I felt utterly miserable. I didn't like where I was. I didn't like what had happened to me. And I didn't like the miserable person I was becoming.

After Mom had left, I looked over at Skye, but she seemed oblivious to her surroundings and had her iPod headphones on. I glanced farther down the ward to see if Amy was awake, but her bed was empty. *She must have gotten up when Mom was here and I didn't notice,* I thought. I reached into the drawer in the cabinet next to me and texted Lois to tell her how unfair everything was. My zodiac phone was lying there. I picked that up. Just looking at it made me angry. I'd sent out a cry for help, and there hadn't even been one reply. *So much for it being a good prize,* I thought, as I picked it up and hurled it to the bottom of my bed. Unfortunately, I misjudged the distance, and it almost hit Amy as she went past before it clattered to the floor. She leaped back in surprise and then looked over at me. She bent over, picked it up, and brought it over to me.

"I am so sorry," I said. "I didn't mean to make you jump."

She smiled and sat on the edge of my bed. "That's

okay. I'm Amy, by the way."

"Marsha."

"You feeling mad about something?" Up close, I could see how pretty she was, with delicate features and big cornflower-blue eyes in a pale face. However, the purple shadows under her eyes, like bruises, showed that she wasn't well.

I nodded. "And then some. I just heard that I can't go home today and well . . . I was just letting off some steam. Sorry. Mom's always telling me that I act before I think and it should be the other way around."

"I know how you feel," she said. "I was mad when I first came in here. It seemed so unfair, like, why me? You should have seen me. I was Queen of Tantrums."

I smiled. She looked so pale and weak that it was hard to imagine her having the energy to have a tantrum.

"But you get your head around it," she continued. "I guess I've gotten more used to it now, and it's not so bad, really."

"What's the matter?" I asked and then put my hand over my mouth. "Oops. Sorry. Me and my big mouth. Not my business."

"I don't mind. I have a type of Hodgkins disease. Something to do with my lymph glands."

"Well, I hope you get better," I said.

She gave me a sad smile. "So do I. There are different

82

types of it. It is treatable, but . . . oh, never mind," she said and then sighed. "It's so boring talking about it."

I glanced over at Skye, who still had her headphones on. "What's she in for?"

"She hurt her ankle. They had to put a pin in it."

"Ouch," I said. "That sounds painful."

Amy nodded. "Yeah. She was pretty fed up about it, too. Apparently she's a dancer—"

"A dancer? Really? So am I. Well, it's one of the things I do. I was supposed to be in the school play. I had the lead role."

"Skye does hip-hop. Apparently she was quite a star. All set to go to some competition until she hurt her leg. I think she was very disappointed. Anyway, better get back to bed. I can't seem to stay up for long these days."

"Give me a nod when you want some company," I said. "I'll come over to hang out."

"That would be nice," said Amy, who then went back to her bed.

I glanced over at Skye. We had more in common than I'd realized. It was a shame she was so standoffish. I turned my attention back to Amy, climbing into her bed. I wished that there was something I could do to help. *Maybe when I am out*, I thought, *I can send her something to cheer her up.*

I sat and read magazines for a short while and tried to resist looking at the clock every five minutes. It was difficult. It kept pulling me like a magnet and then mocking me, like, look at me, look at me. Ha ha. I've hardly moved on at all!

I decided to try my zodiac phone again. *Why not?* I thought. *I have nothing to lose.* I typed in:

```
When I said I needed help, I meant now.
Zodiac Girl
```

The reply was instantaneous.

```
Chill out, Zodiac Girl. Your Mars is conjunct
with the Moon. We will be there soon. Keep
fighting. Mario
```

Not long after, the doors to the room opened and in walked Mr. Ares and a lady who definitely didn't look like one of the nurses. She looked like . . . a mermaid on legs. She was tall and willowy with silvery gray hair in a braid down her back, and she was dressed like a Victorian nanny in a long silver skirt and high-neck jacket. Both of them seemed to know the nurses, and as they talked, they glanced over at me. They looked out of place in the hospital because they radiated light and health. Both Amy and Skye looked up to see Mario as he came over to see me.

He sat on the end of the bed. "So. Marsha. What's all this nonsense?"

"What nonsense?"

"I think you know what I'm talking about."

"No, I don't."

"You haven't stopped moaning since you got in here."

"Me. Wha—? But . . . in case you don't know, I have had an operation on my arm and have been confined to bed. Wouldn't that make most people moan?"

"Some people, yes, but not someone with a chart like yours and not someone who has been chosen to be a Zodiac Girl."

"Oh, that."

"You have your phone and your pendant?"

"Yes. I won them as a prize."

Mario shook his head. "A prize? A PRIZE? You don't get it, do you? It's a lot more than a prize."

"What do you mean?"

"To be a Zodiac Girl means that you're a very lucky girl."

I looked down at my arm. "*Lucky?* Ha! Doesn't seem very lucky to me. In fact, life has been awful since I heard about the Zodiac Girl thing."

"Well, it *is* lucky," said Mario. "Every month, somewhere on the planet, one girl is chosen to be a Zodiac Girl. Only one girl. She gets three things. A piece of jewelry. You got that, right?"

"My pendant with the little ram on it."

"That would be it. She also gets introduced to her guardian, who is me. Me because you're an Aries. Each birth sign has a ruling planet. Mars rules Aries, so you get me."

"Um, could you rewind the tape a mo?" I asked. "I get the ruling planet part. But what do you, the person Mario, have to do with the planet Mars?"

"All the planets are here in human form. I am the living embodiment of Mars."

I burst out laughing. "Yeah, and I'm Queen Nefertiti."

Mario looked offended. "No, you're not. You're Marsha Leibowitz. I know it's a lot to get your head around, but it's true. We all live locally."

"The planets all live locally?"

"Yeah."

"And are here in human form?"

"Yeah."

"Okay . . ." *He is clearly absolutely crazy*, I thought. He is in the hospital to see someone in the psychiatric wing and wandered in here by mistake. "Um, just got to go to the bathroom."

I hopped out of bed and limped over to the nurses' station. "Hey, Cheryl, can I have a moment?" I asked when I saw her sitting and drinking coffee with the lady that Mario had come in with.

"Sure. What is it?"

I beckoned her to come to the door so that the lady wouldn't hear.

"That man by the bed. I think he may have wandered out of the psychiatric wing," I whispered into her ear.

Cheryl laughed. "No. That's Mario. There's no one saner. He does physical therapy here with some of the patients. But the lady I'm having coffee with, she's from the psychiatric department. She's one of the counselors. She visits all the teen patients once or twice a week."

The lady behind waved. "Hi, Marsha. I'm Selene. Cheryl's been telling me all about you."

"Um . . . hi. Um . . . good."

"Marsha!" called Mario. "I haven't finished with you yet!"

I pinched myself as I went back to the bed. Maybe it was me that was going crazy, either that or I was still asleep and having a very weird dream.

"So, Marsha," Mario continued, "I came in today to tell you that you have to change your attitude. Stop feeling sorry for yourself and think good and hard about what is happening to you this month."

"Easy. I can tell you exactly what's happening. I am having a rotten time. All my plans have been ruined."

Mario put his hand to his mouth and yawned.

"Zodiac Girl, get over it. You're bigger than that and you're stronger than that. I am very disappointed to see you behaving like this."

"So how should I be behaving?"

"Like a warrior. Like a leader. Don't you know that Aries is the first sign of the zodiac? People born under your sign become leaders, the movers and shakers of this world. Aries people don't give in, not without a fight."

Although I was indignant that he didn't get how awful my life was at present, a part of me felt like he was speaking to another part of me—a deeper, stronger part—and I couldn't help but respond. I wasn't going to let him know that, though. "Whatever."

"Fine. If that's your attitude, I'm leaving. For each Zodiac Girl it is different. Some use their gift, others ignore it, but remember this: we're here to help."

"Yeah. Planets in human form," I said and put the finger of my good hand up to my temple and made a circle sign as if to say, you're living in Neverland. He turned to walk away. I watched him go back to the nurses' station with Nurse Cheryl and Selene. *I bet they're talking about me now*, I thought, as I saw them get into an animated conversation and Selene glanced over at our section. When I saw Mario sit down, I crept out of bed and then, making sure that I was out of their sight, I positioned myself so I could hear what they were saying while, to anyone in the ward, it looked as if I was casually looking at some of the pamphlets on display.

"Does she know?" asked Selene.

"I think she has some idea," said Nurse Cheryl, "but I don't think she realizes quite what a rough ride she's in for."

"What are her chances?" asked Mario.

"We're not sure. We're keeping her here longer while we do further tests," said Nurse Cheryl.

"Very sad," said Mario. "Poor thing. She has to keep on fighting."

My blood ran cold. *Oh. My. God.* I thought, *They're talking about me. It's worse than I thought. I'm dying. I have to keep on fighting. So that's why Mario came to deliver that little speech.*

I felt faint. *I need to get back to my bed if I don't have long to live,* I thought, scurrying back toward my area before they caught me eavesdropping. *Ohmigod. I wonder if Mom knows. I wonder how long I have.*

Chapter Ten

Selene

I felt numb. Outraged. In shock. One minute I was looking forward to playing the lead role in the school play. My entire life in front of me. Then what seemed like a minor accident, and my life is over. Over before it had even begun. It can't be. There are so many things I want to do. Travel the world. Be a famous actress. Have a boyfriend. I haven't even been kissed yet! I can't die before my first kiss! Preferably with Ollie Blake. (Swoon, swoon.) Tears filled my eyes. I had been looking forward to going home. Counting the hours. Now maybe I will never see our house again.

Do Mom and Dad know? I wondered. *And Lois?* Oh, my dear friend. Who will she hang out with on weekends? Who will she talk to? In my mind's eye, I could see Lois sitting on her own in the school playground. Her face pale. No one to share her lunch with. No one to laugh with. No one to gossip with about what was on TV. About who we had crushes on. Ollie. No one to say "swoon, swoon" with. She'd be lonely without me.

And not just her.

I could see the dining table at home. Mom and Dad, Cissie and Eleanor, and a place set for me. An empty place. An empty chair. No one would be able to eat they'd be so choked up, so sad. And my funeral. A coffin covered in white roses and yellow freesias. Or red roses and ivy? Hmm. I'll decide later. But the whole school will be there. Heads bowed. Someone would probably get a video together of the highlights of my life: when I won the tennis tournament. When I was nine and played the Swan Queen in *Swan Lake*. When I sang a solo in the holiday show in elementary school. It would be so moving for everyone to watch.

What music should I have? Something lighthearted to remind people of some aspect of my character and make them smile? Or something sad with loads of violins to make them cry buckets' worth of tears? Who would get up to talk about me? Dad? Mrs. Pierson? Lois? Not Lois. She wouldn't be able to get any words out, she'd be so upset. It was making me cry just thinking about it. Cut off in her prime, everyone would say. She had everything to live for. She was going to be somebody, that one, but all the good ones die young, don't they? Tears spilled out onto my cheeks at the thought of how moving it would be.

Mario and Selene came out of the nurses' station. I saw Mario look in the direction of my area, and he said something to Selene. She nodded, then he left and she came over. She looked amazing, with silvery-blue eyes in a pale face and the air of someone from a fantasy book about fairies or mermaids.

"Hi there, Marsha. So how are you feeling?" Selene asked.

"Pretty awful. Numb, really."

Selene looked at my wrist. "Numb? Don't worry. The feeling will come back."

"I guess," I said. "It's just I . . . I can't take it in. It doesn't seem fair. I'm trying to get my head around what's happened, but it doesn't seem real."

"Yes. A lot of girls say that when they find out," said Selene.

"Do they? Oh . . ." I didn't know whether to let on that I knew how bad things were because she'd know that I'd been eavesdropping, but I decided why not. If I had only limited time, I may as well be as honest as I could for what was left of it. "Um. I know, you know."

Selene smiled. "Of course I know. And I know you know."

I wasn't sure that she got it. "No. I mean, I know . . ."

"And I know you know," said Selene.

"So you know that I know that you know?"

Selene looked slightly puzzled. "Yes. Of course. Um . . . what are we talking about?"

"About me."

"Being a Zodiac Girl, right?" asked Selene.

"No. That I'm going to die."

"*Die?*" asked Selene, and she sat on the end of the bed. "Oh that."

"Yes. *That*. So it's true?" A feeling of horror came over me as Selene nodded. I'd been half hoping that she was going to tell me that it was all a terrible mistake.

"Well, we're all going to die, aren't we?" said Selene. "There's no avoiding it. One thing is for certain, and that is that we all have to go sometime, but not many girls your age think about it. Most girls your age think they are invincible."

"Ah, but I know that I'm not."

"Well, that makes you a very wise person, Marsha."

"Only because I know."

Selene looked slightly confused. "Yes, you know. Marsha, um . . . what exactly is it you think you know?"

I leaned in toward her so that the others wouldn't hear me. "That my injury is worse than anyone thought. That I may not have long."

"And what makes you think that?"

"I . . . I heard you talking in . . ." I pointed at the nurses' station.

"Ah." Selene nodded. "You heard us talking." Then she laughed. I was shocked. *She's a terrible counselor if she laughs at dying patients*, I thought.

"You're not being very sympathetic, whoever you are. Are you properly qualified?" I asked.

"No one knows more about feelings than I do, Marsha. If you'd actually looked at your zodiac phone, you would know that I am Selene Luna, the Moon."

Another one from the nut club, I thought. I'd had enough of her, whoever she was. I was dying. I wanted real sympathy with soft words, kind looks. Presents.

"Look, Selene," I said, "I don't know what the game is here with the planet theme or whatever. Is it a monthly thing that some crazy doctor dreamed up? Like, let's cheer up the patients by playing dress-up games? Like, last month you were all vegetables, this month you've all decided to be planets. It's fine. It's nice, it's creative, and I am sure some of the patients love it. It cheers them up, distracts them from their problems. We did something similar at our school one year, and on the second Friday of each month we had to go to school dressed as a character out of history. But what is happening to me is major. I don't have time to play games. I am very, very sick."

"No, you're not."

"Yes, I am."

"No. You're not."

"Yes, I am. I heard you saying . . ."

Selene rolled her eyes. "Typical Aries. Always eavesdropping. Always thinking people are talking about you. It's not always about you, you know. There are other signs of the zodiac."

"What do you mean? It's not always about me?"

Selene glanced over at Amy. "We were talking about someone else. Not you."

I glanced over at Amy's bed, where she appeared to be asleep. "Ohmigod. Amy."

Selene nodded. "And we weren't saying that she's going to die, either. She's in for a tough time, but the condition she has is one of the few cancers that is manageable. People hear the word *cancer*, the big C, and think that it automatically means the end. It doesn't. There are so many different types, some curable, some manageable, some, sadly, not. But Amy should come through. It will be a long haul. She has to keep fighting, but the hospital can help her."

I felt so stupid. Embarrassed. Ashamed. And relieved. All in the same moment. "So I am not going to die?"

Selene shook her head. "Yes, you are. I thought we'd established that. Just not any time soon."

"So what are you doing here asking me about my feelings?" I asked and then lowered my voice. "Shouldn't you be over there with . . ."

"Marsha. Don't you get it? Didn't Mario tell you?

You are a Zodiac Girl this month. Girls who are chosen to be Zodiac Girls are picked because either they are at a turning point in their lives or because they have something to learn. Sometimes both. We, the ten planets, are here to assist. My role is to help you get in touch with your feelings because they will guide you. So, once again, Marsha Leibowitz, how are you feeling?"

My brain felt like it was going to explode. I wasn't going to die. But that lovely, gentle girl in the bed across the room might. I could still go home, continue with my life. She might not be able to.

"How am I feeling? How am I feeling? Confused. More confused than I ever have been in my life. In fact . . . I think, I think . . . I may be having a mental breakdown."

Selene laughed again. She was really beginning to annoy me. *Irritation, add that to the pot of feelings*, I thought.

"Breakdown? Excellent," said Selene. "Break down to break through. You'll get there. I'm sure you will. Aries is a strong sign. And don't forget, we're here to help."

With that, she got up to go. I watched her disappear out of the room through the double doors. *So what am I supposed to do or feel?* I asked myself as I glanced back at Amy, who appeared to be sleeping peacefully.

Chapter Eleven

Entertainment

After the excitement of the afternoon visitors, the ward grew quiet and I grew fidgety once again. In my mind, I replayed the conversations that I'd had with Selene and Mario over and over. We're here to help, they'd both said. In that case, I thought, I'll have another look at my phone. I pulled it out and typed in:

Am bored. Zodiac Girl needs entertainment.

Then I pressed SEND. Seconds later, the phone bleeped that I had a message.

Am dispatching the troops. Had to wait until
the planets were aligned in a harmonious way!
Keep fighting. Mario

Five seconds later, the double doors to the room burst open, and in rolled Uri on his unicycle. He was wearing a white doctor's coat and a red nose, and he was juggling bedpans!

My jaw must have fallen open—the whole effect was hysterical. *Ohmigod*, I thought, as he pedaled past, grinning and waving at me a second before catching a flying bedpan.

"Uri!" I called. "Stop it! You'll get into trouble." *Any minute now, security is going to come rushing in and haul him out,* I thought.

"Heard that you were bored," he said as he rolled backward down the room. Skye sat up to watch. Even Amy lifted up her head up a little. The nurses came out of their station and watched with big smiles on their faces. *Why aren't they freaked out?* I wondered, as Uri got off his unicycle and began to juggle mugs from the beverage cart. Four, six, eight in the air. He really was very good at it. After his juggling act, he disappeared into another room, so I couldn't see him. I called Cheryl over.

"What's going on? Why haven't you stopped him?" I asked.

"Why would we? He's Uri. He's a clown doctor. He comes in occasionally to entertain the children and teenagers, and he helps cheer people up."

A bit of a coincidence if you ask me, I thought. *Two seconds after I send out a cry for help, he appears. Hmm?* From the other room, I could hear oohs and ahs and laughter, and it wasn't long before Uri reappeared in our room. He made a low bow, which was very funny because he bent over to his knees then to his feet, then his head seemed to dip past his toes and along the floor as if he was made of elastic. "For our resident Zodiac Girl and her friends," he said and went over to Skye. He got out his stethoscope and put it on the top of her head.

"Hmm," he said as he pretended to listen to her brain. "A very serious problem indeed. Oh dear. Oh dear. Oh dear. I think we need to do a transplant. A . . ." He hesitated and then produced a red nose similar to the one that he was wearing and put it over Skye's nose. She laughed, and Uri pulled a red balloon with something wrapped in a red shiny wrapper on the end of the string from behind her ear. He presented it to her and said, "Belgian chocolate, the very best."

Her face lit up. "My favorite," she said.

Next he went along to Amy's bed. This time he placed his stethoscope over her ear. She giggled.

"Oh my," he said. "What do we have here? I think we need to do a CAT scan to find the source of the problem." From one of his pockets, he produced a black toy cat. "Now lie back."

Amy giggled again and did as she was told while Uri waved the cat at arm's length over her, from head to toe. "Now that's what I call a CAT scan," he said. "Not scary at all, is it?"

Amy shook her head and smiled. Uri stuffed the cat back into his pocket, and then he began to writhe. It looked like there was something alive under his coat. A small moving lump, like a little creature. "Oh. Oh!" cried Uri as he squirmed around. "Someone wants to come and say hello." He pulled a white teddy bear out of nowhere. From thin air. It really was magic because the bear seemed to grow before our eyes. Uri placed the bear next to Amy on the pillow, and then he leaned over and put his stethoscope on the bear's chest and pretended to listen to its heartbeat.

"Uh-huh. Uh-huh," he said and looked at Amy. "This bear has been very sick and very fed up and away from his mommy and daddy bear. He needs lots of cuddles and love. Can you give it to him?"

Amy's eyes glistened with tears. She cuddled the bear close to her and nodded.

And then he came to me. "So. What for the resident Zodiac Girl? Are you missing anything?"

"Um . . . I don't know. Something to do in here?"

"No. No, it's not that. It's . . ." He placed his stethoscope on my arm. "Ah yes. You need a funny bone." He reached into his pockets and pulled out a toy dog bone, large and pink with yellow stars on it. He put it in my hand. "There, that will do the trick. If there are any more problems with the arm, I suggest that you take one of these three times a day."

I decided to play along with him, even though it was all

a little childish. "And how am I supposed to swallow one of those three times a day?"

"Like this," said Uri, and he took the bone, which was as big as my hand, stuffed it into his mouth—miraculously, it went in—swallowed and then opened his mouth to show me that it was empty.

"How? Wha—? How did you do that?"

Uri grinned. "Magic. Now look under your pillow."

I looked under my pillow, and there was the bone. And with it were two miniature bones.

Uri clapped his hands. "And, look, it's had babies! Baby bones." He picked up the two small ones and tossed one to Skye and one to Amy, who were watching with big smiles on their faces. "Here's a spare funny bone for you two in case you ever need one."

"Thanks," said Skye.

"Yeah, thanks," said Amy.

Uri turned back to me and produced a book of crossword puzzles from up his sleeve. "And these are for you to pass the time," he said.

I took the book. I hate crossword puzzles. I tried not to look disappointed because all his other tricks had been really good.

"Um . . . thanks."

"Only joking," he said, and he produced another packet wrapped in silver wrapping paper from his other sleeve.

I ripped off the paper and gasped. It was a portable DVD player and some DVDs: *High School Musical*, *Enchanted*, and *Wall-E*.

"Wow, awesome," I said, because *High School Musical* is one of my all-time favorite movies ever. "Thank you so much."

He indicated Amy and Skye. "Watch them with your new friends. Friends are important wherever you are," he said, and then he robot danced backward through the room. His dancing was very comical, and by this time everyone in my room had big grins on their faces, including the woman with the beverage cart.

"Awesome," I said out loud as Uri did a comical fall and then got up and staggered out through the double doors.

"Yeah," said Skye. "He's cool."

When the atmosphere settled down again, I began to wonder. Was it a coincidence that he'd turned up seconds after my request? Maybe it wasn't. But Cheryl had said that he came by occasionally, so perhaps it just happened to coincide with my text message and had nothing to do with a request on my zodiac phone. Well, there's only one way to find out if there's any connection. I have to try my zodiac cell phone again.

I typed in:

`Am starving for some decent food. Please`

```
send scrumptious supplies.
```

I pressed SEND, and off the message went.

Nothing happened. I kept looking hopefully at the double doors, but the only people who came through were a doctor, a nurse, and a cleaner. I felt my spirits sink again. So Uri's clown-doctor visit had been a coincidence after all. I shifted around and tried to get comfortable. Amy looked like she was asleep, and Skye was listening to her iPod, so I started to watch a DVD. After around ten minutes, the doors opened. A big jolly man bustled in with what looked like a basket of goodies on his left arm.

"Hey, Joe!" called Cheryl.

"Hey there, Nursie," he said and began to dole out little packages in brown paper wrappings. When he got to our section, he gave me a wink.

"I believe you called," he said.

"I . . . I um . . ."

"Mario iz your guardian, yes?" said the man.

"Um, yeah, sort of, um . . . I'm new to all this . . ." I began.

"Zodiac Girl?" he asked.

I nodded, and the man came and leaned over me so that the others couldn't hear him. "I'm Jupiter, but people call me Joe," he whispered. "Best not to let on about ze planet connection, or else people might think you're crazy. Just know that Mario iz on your case, and we're all here for you and will do what we can."

"Oh. Okay, thank you," I said. "And, yes, I sort of know about the planet thing. Theme of the month, right?"

"*Theme?* No. But never mind. Mario iz ze one who has to explain it all."

"He did say something about the planets being here in human form, but . . . you can't have come from a planet. That's impossible, isn't it?"

"Why?" said Joe. "Do you know where you came from?"

"A town down the road."

"I mean before zat. Before you were here as Marsha?"

"Before I was born?"

Joe nodded.

"Um, no, course not. No one does."

"Well, maybe you were from a star," said Joe. "A star up in ze sky."

"Like an alien?"

"No—like energy. But enough of zis kind of talk. I'm not here to give a lecture about where we've come from. Just know zat zere are many things we don't understand, Marsha—many things defy logic—don't close your mind to anything or say something iz not possible. Now, I understand zat you don't approve of ze hospital food so far, yes?"

"Right."

"So what would you like?"

"I love hot chocolate. And I love blueberry muffins. They're my favorite. Dad always gets them for me when I'm sick."

Joe beamed. "Well, izn't zat a coincidence, because I just happen to have . . ." He produced a muffin and a paper mug filled with a steaming liquid. He handed both to me and tapped the side of his nose as if to say that we had a secret between us.

As he left the room to continue down the ward distributing his goodies, I sipped my drink. It was the best hot chocolate I had ever tasted. Thick and creamy with just the right amount of sweetness. And the muffin was melt-in-your-mouth fabulous.

After he'd done his rounds, I called Nurse Cheryl over.

"So where did he come from?" I asked.

"Osbury," she said. "He has a deli there. He pops in when he can with a few things for the patients. There's a whole family of them living and working there, and they come in as volunteers for the hospital from time to time. I wish they could come in more. In fact . . ."

After Joe left, Cheryl announced that someone was coming in from a local beauty salon to do pampering treatments. Half an hour later, a lady named Nessa arrived with two assistants. I couldn't help but stare at her. She looked like a model, no, even more beautiful than that. She looked like a goddess—tall, with blond hair and a perfect heart-shaped face with blue eyes.

"So, who's for bein' pampered?" she asked enthusiastically in a Southern drawl.

Amy, Skye, and I all held up our hands, and the two assistants went to their beds and Nessa came over to mine.

"All right, darlin'?" she asked.

I nodded. "Yes. Actually I'm having an okay day."

She smiled, sat on the end of the bed, peeled back the covers, and began to give me a foot massage. It was pure heaven. While she was doing it, I looked at the names on my phone. Nessa: Venus, it said.

"Are you part of the special club?" I asked.

"What do you mean, darlin'?" asked Nessa. I showed her my phone. "I won this on the Internet, and it has ten names on it. Something to do with astrology and planets."

"That's right," said Nessa. "You're this month's Zodiac Girl, right? Have you met your guardian?"

"Mario, yes, otherwise known as Mars. And um . . . according to my phone, Nessa . . . you're Venus?"

"That's right. Planet of love and beauty. I run a

106

beauty salon in Osbury."

"And you work as a volunteer in the hospital?"

"Sometimes. We all signed up for a bit, to be ready for when you were coming in."

"For me?"

"Yeah, 'cause you're a Zodiac Girl, and we're here to help. Imagine if we told the nursin' staff that we were the planets here in human form. They'd think we were a bunch of crazies and never let us in. We have to think up ways to get around. Ways to be accepted in normal society. It was in your chart that somethin' like this would happen to you, and you might end up in here for a bit, so Mario told us to get ready. To start here as volunteers."

"I can see your point," I said. "Yes, they might think that you were all crazy." *Because you are!* I thought. Either that or my anesthetic hasn't worn off and I am having a strange dream.

Whatever the reason, I don't mind, I thought, after she left and I looked at the clock and saw that three hours had passed since they arrived. *Are they volunteers with overactive imaginations who are a little bonkers? Or not?* I wondered. *If not, it's like having the modern-day equivalent of an Aladdin's lamp.* I felt a rush of excitement flood through me as I considered what else the zodiac phone might be able to do.

Chapter Twelve

My bee-ootiful sisters

"Why are you crying? And what the heck happened to your hair?" asked Cissie that evening when she arrived with Mom and Eleanor, and I burst into tears at the sight of them. The three of them looked so pretty and familiar when they walked in that I couldn't help it. Skye glanced up at them. People always stared at my sisters because they were so striking, and they looked especially so in the brightly-lit room. Cissie had obviously just come from ballet class and was dressed in fuchsia leggings and a pink T-shirt. Eleanor was wearing a tiny denim skirt over thick black tights. She had the longest legs and knew how to show them off.

"I'm just so pleased to see you," I replied. "I . . . I thought I'd never see you again."

Eleanor sat down on a chair to the right of my bed. "Why not? You're such a drama queen, Marsha. You only hurt your wrist. Now, when I was in the hospital, it really was serious. Remember, Mom? When I fell off my horse. The doctors thought I'd never walk again."

"Yes—" Mom began.

"Nonsense," said Cissie as she sat on a chair to the left of my bed. "It was a sprain, nothing more, but, when I was in the hospital after my fall, the doctors thought I might have damaged my brain—"

"You did. No doubt about it," said Eleanor, and she made a face at Cissie.

Mom settled herself on the end of the bed. "Now, girls," she said.

"As I was saying," Cissie interrupted in a raised voice. "I had a concussion. Now that is serious."

"Nonsense," said Eleanor. "They didn't even keep you in overnight."

Normally, I would have joined in with gusto. It was always like this with my sisters, each one of us competing to outdo the others, whatever was at stake. Our voices would get louder and louder in the fight to be heard. But today it felt like my birthday, like Christmas, like the most special *special* day because I'd had a lovely morning and I wasn't going to die. At least not yet. I sat there beaming at my gorgeous sisters and my beautiful mother.

"What's the matter, Marsha?" asked Cissie. "You're looking at us strangely."

"Yeah. Are you on drugs?" asked Eleanor.

"No. Just really, really pleased to see you. I had forgotten how beautiful you all are."

"She's definitely on drugs," said Cissie.

"You know, guys, I really love you," I said.

"Whoa! Maybe you did damage more than your wrist," said Eleanor. "Mom, she's lost her mind."

Mom smiled at me. "Not at all. I think that's sweet, Marsha, and we love you, too."

"No, we don't," chorused Cissie and Eleanor, but they looked slightly dewy-eyed when they said it.

"So what did happen to the hair?" asked Eleanor.

I put my hand up to my head. I was longing to wash it. "It was for a part in the school play. Ice Queen," I replied.

Mom patted my hand. "Marsha got the part, didn't you, dear? But um . . . she can't do it now."

I suddenly realized that I didn't mind about not playing the Ice Queen anymore. I was going to live. I was going to get out of the hospital. There would be other parts. Other plays. "It's okay," I said. "There are more important things."

"That's the attitude," said Mom, but she looked surprised.

"So, kid, when are you getting out of here?" asked Cissie.

I was in such a good mood that I didn't even mind that she'd called me kid. Usually that would have started a full-blown argument because she knows that I hate it. "Tomorrow, if everything's okay. In fact, Mom, they fixed the x-ray machine, and I had mine redone just before you came in. When Dr. Sam's had a chance to look at it, which the nurses think will be in the morning, I'm out of here."

"Cool," said Cissie, and she split the goodies that Mom had brought in and proceeded to help herself to the chocolates. "No point in letting these go to waste, then."

Eleanor opened one of the magazines and began to read. "And you'll be able to read these at home, so I may as well have a look now since I'm busy the rest of the week."

I didn't even mind that. "Help yourself," I said. "Help yourself."

On the other side of the ward I saw Amy glance over and smile. I smiled back at her.

As soon as the visitors had left for the evening, I got out of my bed and went over to Amy's. Her arm was attached to some type of drip. She was awake and saw me looking at it. "Blood transfusion," she said. "Sometimes they give me one before they start my chemotherapy. You'll see me change color as it goes through. I go from pale to pink."

"How long are you in for?" I asked.

"Only three days this time. I come in once every three weeks for a couple of days, and they do my treatment. I'm on round four. Two more to go."

"Then what?"

Amy shrugged. "Don't know exactly. More treatment."

I looked at the blood bag. "Does that make you feel weird?"

Amy shook her head. "Nah. Makes me feel better. It's the chemo that makes me feel weird. After it, I have one week of feeling awful, one week of feeling medium awful, and one week of feeling almost all right, and then I have to come back and start the process all over again."

"It must be terrible. You poor thing."

Amy shrugged and glanced away.

"God. Sorry. Me and my big mouth. Just say if you don't want to talk about it."

"I don't want to, if you don't mind. It's . . . it's boring. I'd like to hear about you, though. Tell me all about you and why you're in here."

"No probs," I said with a grin. "Permission . . . no, an invitation to talk about myself. You don't know what you've let yourself in for." For the next ten minutes, I filled her in on all the events of the last few days, aside from the eavesdropping part.

"I bet you would have made a great Ice Queen," she said.

"Yeah. But I guess not many Ice Queens have a great big plaster cast on their arm."

Amy laughed and then looked at me kindly. "You looked a little upset before. Did you . . . Did you . . . have some bad news that you haven't told me about?"

"Uh . . ." For a moment I felt lost for words. How could I tell her that I had been upset, but only because I thought

112

what was happening to her was happening to me? And what a relief it had been when I'd found out it wasn't me after all. I so wished I could give her some news. Like that I was a good fairy and could wave a magic wand to make whatever was wrong with her go away. "No biggie. It's just so boring in here. Like the hours seem to stretch out until forever."

Amy rolled her eyes. "Tell me about it. Some hospitals have recreation rooms where there are things to do, but not this one. It wasn't in the budget, apparently."

"Oh, yeah. I remember now. A girl at my school was trying to organize a charity event to raise money for a recreation wing. She was looking for people to perform." Now that I'd met Amy and experienced for myself how endless days in the hospital could be, I felt ashamed of the way that I had turned Sophie down. I decided that I'd better change the subject before Amy asked if I was going to be in Sophie's show and realized what a selfish cow I was. "But come on—fair's fair. I've told you about me. What about you?"

"Not a lot to tell. I'm thirteen. One sister who lives in Australia. Music is my thing. I like all types. Um. Got sick around six months ago. Boring boring, don't want to talk about it. Wish it hadn't happened. Felt it wasn't fair. There are so many things I still want to do, and having to come back here again and again really gets in the way. I moaned and groaned a lot, but now I think, what's the point? I try to get on with it, make the best I can of it. Get in here, get out as fast as poss. Know what I mean?"

"Oh, yeah. But you'll be out soon."

"For a while. It's part of my life now, and I just have to accept that. I try not to feel sorry for myself, though, of course some days I do."

"Well, I think you're amazing. If it was me, I'd be a total mess."

Amy smiled. "No you wouldn't. You deal with it day by day."

At that moment, the nurse came over to change Amy's drip, and she shooed me away.

"Laters," I said. "Want to watch a DVD when they're finished with you?"

Amy beamed back at me. "Yeah. What do you have?"

"*High School Musical* and *Enchanted*."

Amy gave me a thumbs-up as the nurse swished the curtains around her.

On the way back to my bed, I looked over to see Skye. I thought that I might ask her to join us, but she had her headphones on and her eyes closed, so I decided it was best not to disturb her. As I climbed back into my own bed, I felt so thankful that this really would be the last night and soon I'd be free.

Chapter Thirteen

Going home

Stepping out from the hospital lobby the next morning into the light of the parking lot felt like emerging from a bad dream. All the colors in the outside world seemed more vivid, all the sounds louder.

I spotted Mom's car immediately. Silly thing—she'd tied a bunch of pink balloons onto the back. I gave her a hug to show her that I appreciated the gesture.

Mom supported my arm while I hobbled over to the car and got into the passenger seat. As she started up the car and drove through the traffic, I gazed out the window. It felt so good to actually be going home—to be back in the world where things were happening.

The drive to our house took around 20 minutes, and when Mom opened our front door, I felt like I was being let into paradise. Everything was how I remembered but somehow brighter and more comfortable-looking. I inhaled the familiar smell of charred toast and strawberry—from the scented candles that Cissie always burned in her room. Yummy. We went through to the kitchen, and there on the table was a chocolate cake with shiny, glistening frosting.

"Cissie and Eleanor stayed up and baked it for you last night after they got back from the hospital," said Mom. "Chocolate fudge, your favorite."

She cut us each a piece, and we sat at the kitchen table to eat them with tall glasses of milk. I looked over at Mom and smiled at her. "This is the happiest day of my whole life," I said.

Mom laughed. "Let's see how long that feeling lasts," she said.

"Oh, it will, it will," I said. "I will never take anything here for granted ever again."

Mom raised an eyebrow as if to say that she still didn't believe me.

After the cake, I wandered upstairs and stuck my head in all the rooms as if I was going around the house for the first time. Our lovely white bathroom that smelled of jasmine soap instead of antiseptic, like the shampoo that Nurse Abbie had used to wash my hair at the hospital this morning. How could I have ever thought our house was too small? It was perfect. Next was Cissie's room, with the cornflower-blue walls and all her posters of famous ballet dancers. Farther along the hallway was Eleanor's room, painted baby pink but now covered in so many posters of bands that you could hardly see the walls. It was chaos as usual in there, with drawers and closets open—their contents spilling out, bottles of nail polish and makeup strewn across her dressing table.

"Lovely, lovely," I said. Both rooms looked so comfy. At the back next to my room was Mom and Dad's. I opened the door. It felt so peaceful in there. A white bedspread and curtains and lavender walls with a neat pile of books on both their sides of the bed. History books on Dad's side; gardening books, cookbooks, and magazines on Mom's.

And, at last, my own room looking out over the backyard.

"Hello, room," I said as I opened the door. I went and sat for a moment on the window seat, looking out over the lawn covered in orange and gold leaves that had fallen from the trees. Then I got up and sat on my bed, sighing at how comfortable it felt. I lay back. "Ahhhhh, wonderful bed. I love you. I've missed you," I said, sinking back. I fell into a light sleep, only to be woken by the sound of the doorbell. A few minutes later, Lois appeared at my door. She bounded over and was about to give me a huge hug when she remembered my arm.

"Whoops," she said. "How is it? How does it feel?"

"Better," I said. "It's okay, but I feel fanlubblytastic."

"Why? What's happened? Has anything happened with the zodiac people?"

I filled her in on all their comings and goings in the

hospital, and her eyes grew large with amazement. "Awesome," she said.

"Yeah. Apparently Mario, my guardian, got them all to be volunteers especially for me."

"You're so lucky," said Lois. "So now what?"

I shrugged.

At that exact moment, the zodiac phone rang in my pocket. I pulled it out. It was Mario.

"Zodiac Girl," he said.

"Mario," I replied in exactly the same somber tone and gave Lois a thumbs-up. She grinned back at me.

"You're out?"

"I'm out."

"You know what you have to do now?"

"Yes. Have a great big bubble bath. Mom's cooking my favorite lunch, then a bit of TV."

"No. Wrong answer."

"Why not? I just got home."

"I know. But what are you going to do next?"

"I don't know. Um . . . get better. Go back to school?"

"Marsha," said Mario in an exasperated tone of voice. "Can't you get it through your thick skull? You are an Aries. Aries are the movers and shakers of the zodiac."

"That's me. So?"

"They are the leaders. The ones that make things happen. What are you going to make happen?"

Lois was making faces at me. "What's he saying?"

I shrugged my shoulders and made a face as if to say, I didn't know.

"Mario, can't you just tell me if I am supposed to do something?"

"No, I can't. It has to come from you, and I would have thought that it was obvious by now."

"Give me a clue," I said.

"*Clue?* CLUE!" he roared. "That's all you've had since your time started. I don't know. I really don't. Haven't you learned anything?"

"Yeah. That I don't like being in the hospital. That's what I learned."

I could hear Mario sigh in a weary way on the other end of the phone. "Look," he said. "Sleep on it, why don't you?"

"Sounds like as good a plan as any," I said, and he sighed again and then hung up.

"What?" asked Lois.

"I don't know. He says I am supposed to do something. That I am a leader." I caught a glimpse of my reflection. I still looked weird with my brittle white hair. "Maybe that I shouldn't have dyed my hair? Maybe I should get a new style?"

Lois giggled and nodded.

Chapter Fourteen

Back to business

Thump, thump, thump. Someone was banging on the bathroom door. "Marsha! Get a move on. What are you doing in there? Taking a nap?" Cissie yelled.

Another thump, and then Eleanor's voice. "Yeah. There's a line out here. You're not the only one who has to get ready and out this morning."

"Give me a break," I said, opening the door. "It's not easy with only one arm, you know, and a sore ankle."

"*Not easy with ownwee one arm,*" my horrible sisters chorused together, while making silly faces at me.

"You two have no idea what it is like to live in pain," I said as I pushed past them. They didn't. Even the simplest of tasks, like getting dressed, is hard with only one working arm. Luckily, my ankle was feeling a lot better—almost back to normal—but I wasn't going to tell them that.

They both doubled over laughing. Cissie held the back of her palm up to her forehead. "You haf no idea vot it is like to lif in pain," she said in a stupid fake Russian spy accent. "My life is so trageek." Eleanor took advantage of Cissie being distracted to get into the bathroom and shut the door behind her.

"Hey! I was next!" cried Cissie as soon as she realized, and then the thumping on the door began again.

"Be quiet out there!" Dad called from the bedroom.

Indie music was blasting in Eleanor's bedroom, world music from Cissie's, and I could hear the radio on down below in the kitchen.

"This house is SO noisy!" I said, heading back into my bedroom. "And TOO small."

It hadn't even been a week since I had left the hospital, and it was back to business as usual. My sisters' sympathy had lasted around 24 hours, about as long as the chocolate fudge cake that they had baked for me—and that they polished off when they got home from school. It had been good being back at school for the first few days—I had been the center of attention, and everyone had wanted to sign my cast. But they soon lost interest and moved on to other things, like the school play. The hurt that I couldn't play the Ice Queen had soon come back when I saw that Carol Kennedy was playing my part.

I'd tried to talk Mrs. Pierson into letting me do the part with my injured arm and ankle. I said that it would show what a liberal school we were—letting the less than fortunate take main parts. She smiled, patted me on the head, and called me sweetheart, which made me ANGRY.

I had bumped into Mario a few times in the hallway near the gym, and each time he asked me the same thing: "Got it yet, Zodiac Girl?"

Each time, I gave him the same reply. "Nope."

I wasn't being difficult. I really didn't know what he was talking about.

"Marsha, are you ready?" Mom called up the stairs. Her sympathy hadn't lasted long, either—once she knew that I wasn't going to die, she had soon reverted to being her usual bossy self.

So much for being a Zodiac Girl, I thought, as I struggled into my jacket. All the treats and fun of that had dried up as soon as I'd gotten home, aside from one text message saying that Mercury was retrograde, so it would be a quiet time for a week or so.

"Almost!" I called back. It was time for my first physical therapy session at the hospital.

The physical therapy wing was in a separate part of the hospital from where I was before. It was a modern building with plenty of light streaming in through tall windows.

"This is nice, isn't it?" said Mom, as we made our way to the waiting room. "Not as depressing as that other place."

"I just hope it doesn't hurt," I said, hobbling along.

Mom hugged me. "It will help," she said.

There was only one other person in the waiting room when we got there. Skye. Despite her being so cool with me when we were in the hospital room, I felt pleased to see her. We had shared an experience that no one else— especially my sisters—could understand. She glanced over and jutted out her chin. I suppose that was her way of saying hi.

"Hey," I said. "You're out."

She nodded. "Time off for good behavior."

Mom went off to find the bathroom, so I sat down next to Skye.

"How's it been?" I asked.

She shrugged. "Better than being in here," she said.

"Ditto. My own pillows. My own bed."

"Been up to see Amy?" she asked.

I shook my head. I hadn't even thought about Amy in the last few days. I felt ashamed. "No. I um . . . I thought she went home in between her treatments."

"Not this time," said Skye. "Something to do with her white blood cell count being low and her immune system being weak, so they wanted to keep an eye on her."

"Poor thing," I said. "I'll go up after the physical therapy."

Skye nodded and then got out her iPod and put the headphones in her ears. I got the message. Conversation over. I found my magazine and started to read. After half an hour, a nurse called Skye's name and mine.

Skye hobbled up. I stayed where I was.

"Must be a mistake," I said. "I'll wait here."

Skye nodded and then shuffled off down the corridor and disappeared into a side room. Moments later, the nurse called again. "Marsha Leibowitz."

"You'd better go, dear," said Mom.

I got up and made my way along the corridor and into the room where Dr. Sam was sitting. Skye was standing over by the window.

"Hey, Marsha. How's the arm and the ankle?" he asked.

"Good. Both a little stiff."

"Then this will be timely. Now, I bet you're wondering why I've asked you both in here together."

I nodded, and Skye glared at him.

"Well, Marsha, there's not a lot we can do for your wrist at this stage, so today will be about your ankle continuing to improve. Your physical therapy is going to be really similar to Skye's, and it's always more fun to do it with a pal, so I thought I'd put you both in together."

Skye and I exchanged unenthusiastic glances. If she was going to continue being unfriendly, then so was I.

Dr. Sam left the room, and a lady in a white coat came in and introduced herself as Martha. She asked us to stand up and she then put us through a series of exercises. It felt good to do the rotations and stretches, but I could see that Skye was finding it more difficult. I glanced at her at one point, and her face looked strained and pale.

"Take it easy, Skye," said Martha.

Skye grimaced. "Yeah, don't try to run before I can walk," she said.

"Something like that," said Martha.

Mom was waiting for me when we got out.

"Ready to go?" she asked.

I shook my head. "Can you give me a few minutes? I want to go up to see someone in the other ward."

"Sure," said Mom. "I'll go and grab a coffee from the cafeteria."

We made our way over to the main hospital building, and Mom left me at the elevator. I didn't have to wait long, and soon I was back in the ward. It felt strange being there again, and I felt a strong sense of relief that I wasn't going to have to stay this time.

Nurse Cheryl came out of the nurses' station. "Hey, if it isn't our little marshmallow. How are you, Marsha?"

"Great," I said. "At least, okay. I came to see Amy. Is she still here?"

Nurse Cheryl nodded and looked over to the room that I'd been in. "She's been missing you girls, I think."

I crossed over to the room where I'd stayed and saw that there was only one bed that was occupied, and that was Amy's. She appeared to be asleep, and I was about to leave when she opened her eyes and her face lit up. "Marsha," she said. "I'd been hoping that you might come back. Skye was in earlier." She sat up and patted the end of the bed. "How are you?"

I glanced over at the empty beds. "I'm doing fine, thanks, but . . . isn't there anyone else in here with you?"

She shook her head. "No. The nurses say it's wonderful and quiet now, but . . ." Her eyes filled with tears. "It's been awful, especially at night. I know we didn't talk much when you were in and Skye kept to herself most of the time, but at least you were there. I knew there was someone in the other beds, and I didn't feel so alone."

I reached out and took her hand. I felt like my heart was going to break. I was free, but she was still in here, away from her family and home. "What about during the day? Has the clown doctor been in?"

Amy shook her head. "I asked about him, but apparently there's just him, and he goes around to a few hospitals, not just this one. One of the nurses told me that they didn't have the budget for entertainment." She smiled. "He was great, though, wasn't he? He really took my mind off things for a while."

I nodded, and then I had an idea. I got up and did the funny dancing that I used to do when I was younger to entertain relatives at Christmas. It's a bit of moonwalking and then robot dancing. As I was dancing, I didn't notice that Skye had come in and was standing behind me. I noticed Amy looking over my shoulder, so I turned around. Skye gave me one of her chin-jut nods. I jutted my chin back at her.

"Not bad, newbie," she said. "Don't let me stop you." She started counting time by snapping her fingers, so I started dancing again. Slowly, Skye came over and began to move in time with me, mostly her upper body, but she could move her feet a little with the help of her crutches. Despite her injured ankle, I could see that she had natural rhythm and could dance, even if a little slowly because of her foot. It was as if we tuned into each other and went into this spontaneous routine.

When we'd finished, Amy clapped. "Excellent," she said. "Hip-hop heroines."

"Yeah, cool," said Skye.

I grinned back at her. "Thanks." I turned back to Amy. "Hey, I have to go now. My mom is waiting downstairs, but I will come back and visit."

"Promise?"

"Promise," I said.

"And I can stay a while longer," said Skye. "My

mom's not picking me up for another fifteen minutes."

"Great," said Amy.

"Laters," said Skye, and for the first time, she smiled at me.

"Laters," I said.

That night before I went to sleep, I checked my zodiac phone, and there was a message from Mario:

Time is running out, have you got it yet?

I got into bed and lay staring at the ceiling. *Got what? Got what?* I asked myself. I couldn't concentrate for long, though. I couldn't stop thinking about Amy. I was home, comfy, and in familiar surroundings. She was still in the hospital, and although the staff were really nice and did what they could, I knew that it felt strange at night with the distant noises down the corridors and comings and goings in the ward. And then it was as if a light bulb flashed on in my head. That was it! That was what Mario had been waiting for. I climbed out of bed, got my zodiac phone, and replied to his message.

Got it. I know exactly what I have to do!

Chapter Fifteen

It's showtime, folks

You want to do *what?*" asked Dad, as my family sat around having breakfast on Saturday morning.

"I need to raise around . . . um, a million dollars should do it," I said.

Dad almost spat out his coffee. Mom, Cissie, and Eleanor burst out laughing.

"Give the girl credit for having a goal," said Mom.

"Yeah. But . . . how exactly are you going to get this million dollars?" Cissie asked.

"Okay, maybe not a million, then. Maybe just around five hundred grand. I haven't actually researched my figures yet."

Everyone started laughing again like I was telling the best jokes ever. "Not researched my figures yet," Cissie mimicked in a silly voice.

Dad was the first one to make an attempt to straighten his face. "Sorry, Marsha. We shouldn't be laughing. Now explain what all this is about."

"You can laugh. You'll see. I'm an Aries, and we're the

leaders of the zodiac, in case you didn't know. The movers and shakers. We make things happen," I said.

"So what are you going to make happen?" asked Eleanor.

"I am going to raise enough money to build a recreation wing at the hospital so that children and teenagers in there can go and chill out or play on computers or listen to music or paint or whatever they feel like. I also need to fund a regular bunch of entertainers to go in for those who can't get out of bed."

Hah! That shut them up.

"Wow! Good for you," said Mom. "But don't you think that's maybe a bit ambitious?"

I shook my head and quoted back our principal's favorite quote: "We have to reach for the stars."

Cissie giggled and grabbed her purse, which was on the counter behind us. She pulled out her wallet and handed me a coin. "There's a quarter, kid," she said, and she and Eleanor started laughing again.

I got up to leave. "I should have known better than to expect you lowlifes to take me seriously."

"We do, sweetheart," said Mom, "but you have to think this through a little."

"I know that," I said. "I'm not stupid. I am going to figure out a business plan."

Dad was doing his best to keep a straight face, but he

couldn't do it. I gave him a mean look.

"No, no," he spluttered. "I think it's great. You make me very proud."

"I am going to change the world. You'll see," I said, and I left the room, slamming the door behind me so that there was no doubt about how I felt.

Lois was more understanding.

"Great. So how are you going to do that?" she asked after I'd told her my plan over the phone. I looked down at the blank page in the notebook in front of me. "Um . . . Well . . . Do you have any ideas?"

"Um . . . No."

"Okay. No problem. Let's go to the library. There must be a book on how to make millions. Meet you there in half an hour."

Our public library was only around the corner from where we lived, and I got there before Lois. I decided to call Mario while I stood outside waiting. He sounded pleased to hear from me.

"Hi, Zodiac Girl. I got your message. So you know what to do?"

"Yep. Raise money for a recreation wing at the hospital."

I heard a sharp intake of breath, and then he

chuckled. "Okay. Good. How much are you aiming for?"

"Around a million."

I heard another sharp intake of breath. "Good. Good to be ambitious."

"Is that what you were waiting to hear?" I asked.

"Sort of. It's always up to the individual Zodiac Girl to decide what she's going to do with her month. Some do a lot, some do very little. With you being an Aries, I knew it would be something extraordinary but, as I said, it had to come from you. So, no, it wasn't exactly what I was waiting to hear."

"So how do I do it?"

"Ah. Now that has to come from you, too."

"I thought I was supposed to have won a prize or something? And part of that is your help?"

"Right. But you're an Aries. You have to lead."

I was beginning to get impatient. "You're not being very helpful."

"I will be when you tell me what to do."

"Okay, which one of your team has anything to do with finance?"

"That would be Jupiter, which is the planet of expansion, so if it's favorably aspected in your chart, it can mean winnings of some type, since everything it touches expands. And then Pluto is sometimes known as the Lord of Wealth, so get those two together in a chart, and it could be good, depending on where they are."

"Can you look at my chart and see where they are?"

"Can do. I'll get back to you. Wait until you've heard from me, though, okay?"

I could see Lois coming down the sidewalk, and I waved. "Okay. Maintain radio contact, Mario. We're not through yet."

"Glad to hear it," he said and hung up.

Lois linked her arm through my good one, and we went into the library and up to the desk where a tall, thin lady with a wrinkly neck was busy stamping books.

"Excuse me," I said. "Where are the reference books?"

"What type?" she asked me without looking up.

"The ones on how to make a lot of money."

She looked up then with an amused glint in her eye. "You need to be more specific," she said. "You mean like what career can make you money?"

"No. Now. I need to raise about a million, soon, maybe five hundred grand."

"Don't we all, dear," she said and jerked her chin toward a small room off the main part of the library. She looked like she was having a hard time not laughing. "You might find something in there. Let me know if you find anything good." And she went back to her stamping.

I rolled my eyes. "What is wrong with people that they

all find this so funny?"

Lois shrugged. "Yeah. They don't know you, do they?"

"Don't you think I could do it?"

"I think when you set your mind to something, you go for it," she replied.

I pointed up at the sky and did a small kung fu leap into the air. "Huzzah! Zodiac Girl, watch out, she's coming."

"Shhh," shushed an old man, who was sitting and reading a newspaper.

"Sorry," I whispered back. Lois and I tiptoed into the reference section and began to search the shelves.

After half an hour of hauling books down and flicking through the pages, looking for any kind of clue on how to make money fast, I turned to Lois.

"Anything?"

She glanced up from the heavy book that she had in front of her and shook her head. "Corporate this, corporate that, and a load of graphs I don't understand, but no make-money-quick schemes. What have you found?"

"Nothing. I don't think we are going to find the answer here. Let's go and get a juice down the road and rethink the plan."

Lois saluted. "Aye, aye, captain."

We made our way out of the library and along the main street. It was a gray day outside, so we hurried along, eager to get out of the cold. Just before we turned into the doorway at the Juicy Juice bar, a poster in the window caught my eye. Lucky Lotto scratch cards. That was the answer. Spend five dollars, and the prize was one million dollars. And Mario had said something about Jupiter, hadn't he? Something about everything it touched meaning expansion. Well, you couldn't get a better expansion than five dollars into a million. I just knew that I was going to win.

"How much money do you have on you, Lois?"

Lois put her hand in her pocket. "Four dollars and fifty cents."

"And I have five dollars and fifty cents." I pointed at the poster for the cards.

"Oh no, we shouldn't," she said. "My mom said never to waste money on those."

"Someone has to win," I said. "And I can feel that it's going to be me, I mean, us. I can feel it in my bones. It's just the amount we need. We could get two. Two tries, double our luck."

Lois looked unenthusiastic. "But then we wouldn't be able to get a drink, and I'm thirsty."

"Sacrifices have to be made in the line of honor," I said. I didn't quite know what I meant, but it

135

sounded good.

"And now you're making me feel guilty," Lois said with a moan.

"Don't be such a moaner," I said. "Guilt is good. It means you have a conscience and are really a good person. Now hand over your money."

Lois gave me her money, but she didn't look happy about it.

"Oh, come on, Lois, cheer up. In this life, there are winners and losers, and we, my dear, are winners."

"If you say so," said Lois, and with a look of regret back at the juice bar, she turned and trudged after me into the drugstore.

I marched up to the counter behind which was a young man who was busy watching a football game on the TV screen to the right of the register.

"Two five-dollar scratch cards," I said in my best confident voice.

It seemed like a particularly exciting moment was happening on the screen, and the man barely glanced at me. He peeled off two cards, all the while keeping his attention on the game. "Oh!" he cried, as one of the players tumbled to the ground after a fierce tackle.

I handed him the money, which he put into the register as if he was on automatic pilot. We were about to leave the store when he called after me, "Hey. How old are you?"

"Sixteen," I said in a deep voice. "But the cards are not for me, anyway. They're for my sister for her twenty-first birthday. I thought they'd make an unusual gift."

The man was hardly listening as one of the players ran the ball down one side of the field. As I opened the door to leave, I heard him cry out at the TV, "Go, go GOOOOOO!"

I shut the door behind us and grinned at Lois. "Well, that was easy! I thought for a minute that he wasn't going to sell us the cards."

"But you told a lie. Your sisters are sixteen and eighteen."

"White lie," I said. "There's a difference, and it's for a good cause."

Lois pointed at a bus stop over by a church in front of the park. "Let's go over there."

We made our way over to the bench and sat down, ready to scratch our cards.

"I feel so excited," I said. "Don't you?"

"A little," said Lois. "Give me one, then, seeing as I paid for it."

I handed her a card and looked down at mine. "Okay. Ready, set . . . go."

And we started scratching. There were four games on the card. On the first, you had to match the winning symbol. I scratched off the winning symbol. It was the letter K. I scratched off the rest. Four letters appeared. N, P, R, and X. No K.

"Bummer," I said. "How did you do?"

Lois shook her head. "No match."

"Well, we have three left," I said and began to scratch the rest of the card. In the next game if the amount in the left-hand column under the title "YOURS" was higher than the amount in the middle column under "THEIRS," you won the prize in the third column. We got busy scratching.

YOURS	THEIRS	PRIZE
14	18	$20
23	30	$100,000
34	45	$500
38	39	$1,000,000

"Oh!" I cried as I scratched off the last amounts. "I almost won. Thirty-eight, thirty-nine, a million!"

"Almost doesn't make it," said Lois. "I didn't win, either."

We started on the third game. Match three amounts to win. I scratched off $40, $400, $50, $400. "Ooh, ooh, I just need one more four hundred," I said as I continued scratching. But no luck. The other amounts were $4 and $25.

"One last game," I said. "This has to be it. Come on,

Jupiter, my man. Work your magic."

The last game was like a slot machine in that you had to get a row of three of the same. I scratched away. Two cherries and a lemon. Two apples and an orange. Two oranges and a cherry. A peach and two lemons. I checked and checked all the games. I could not believe it. I hadn't won a thing.

"Ohmigod, ohmigod," said Lois as she got to her last row. "Cherry, cherry, ohmigod, cherry! Marsha, I won. I WON!"

I felt a blast of adrenaline flood through me. "How much? How much? Scrape off the prize."

Lois quickly scraped off the last box, and her face fell. "A . . . a dollar! Oh no. Is that all?"

"Give it to me. That can't be right," I said and checked her card for mistakes, but there it was: one dollar.

"Well, at least I can go and claim it, and maybe we can get a can of soda to share."

"Okay," I said. "Or . . . or maybe you could buy one of those dollar scratch cards. Maybe we could still win."

Lois gave me a withering look. "Marsha, leave it. You stay here while I go to claim our winnings." She set off toward the store, and while I sat waiting, my zodiac phone bleeped.

"Hello?" I said.

"Marsha?"

"Yeah."

"Mario. Today there's a good link to Saturn, but there are no good aspects from Jupiter. In fact, it's at a bit of a difficult angle."

"Too late."

"What do you mean?"

"I just gambled and lost."

"But I told you not to do anything until you heard from me."

"I . . . I have to go. My friend's coming back."

Lois didn't look happy. "The man in the store wouldn't even give me our dollar. He said you'd said you were going to give the cards to your sister and you lied. He said never to go in there ever again, or he'll call the police."

"So not even a drink?"

"No," said Lois as she sat down beside me. "I told you so. And now I hate you."

Chapter Sixteen

Moneymaking ventures

When a bus came, two minutes later, Lois got on it. I didn't even bother to get up to go with her. I'm not speaking to her anymore. She hates me. *Life sucks*, I thought, as I watched the bus drive off. At least Lois had her bus pass with her. I left mine at home and would have to call Mom if I didn't want to walk the two miles to get home. And how was I going to explain that I didn't have any money?

As I was sitting there contemplating my next move, I saw a familiar figure coming across the park toward me. It was that weird principal who'd been so rude to me in the waiting area of the hospital. *The last person I want to see*, I thought. I pulled the hood of my jacket over my head and looked down at the ground in the hope that he'd keep on going.

"If it isn't our little Zodiac Girl," I heard him say moments later.

I kept staring at the ground. "Nff. Not me. Must be mistaken."

Dr. Cronus sat down next to me. "How is your wrist?"

I decided that there was no point in hiding. He clearly knew who I was. "Still a little sore. Why do you ask? Did you come to gloat again?"

Dr. Cronus sighed. "Not at all. Not at all. No. Mario told me what you want to do. I've been looking at your birth chart, and you're a fiesty young thing—I can see that."

"Yeah. Aries, the movers and shakers of the world."

Dr. Cronus looked at me almost kindly. It was very unsettling. "You're feeling dispirited, aren't you?" he asked. "Weary and misunderstood."

I nodded. "That's exactly how I feel. I . . . so wanted to do something good. To help at the hospital I was in, but . . . well, everything's gone wrong."

"No need to exaggerate to make your point. Surely *everything* has not gone wrong?"

"I need a million dollars, and what do I do? I lose the only money I had by senseless gambling."

Dr. Cronus nodded somberly. "Yes, that was foolish. But you've learned now that there are no easy ways to make money."

"Tell me about it. So. Mario said the people in his planet club will help me. That was the prize. Help. Can you help?"

"*Planet club?* What's this nonsense?"

"You know. You all pick a planet to be. Nessa's Venus. You chose Saturn. Mario is Mars. Actually, I was wondering about that. On my phone, it says there are ten of you. Is that the whole club? Like, what if someone wants to join and also be a Venus planet? What happens then?"

"There are ten planets. Individual. Unique."

"That limits your membership, Dr. Cronus. Like, I don't know how you fund your club, but I am sure there are costs. Maybe that's how I could make some money. Advertise your club a little, get you a few new members— people who like pretending to be a planet, like you guys. Sounds like it could be fun. Do you have special nights? You know, when you all get together? Themed dinners? Picnics? That sort of thing?"

Dr. Cronus was looking at me as if I had grown an extra head. "You don't seem to have exactly grasped the situation. We are the living embodiment of the planets. We are the real thing. I am Saturn. I am not *pretending* to be him, he scoffed."

I could not stop myself from laughing. "You're good, Doctor, really good. And I'll play along; I like a game as much as anyone. But, seriously, how can you guys help me achieve my aim?"

Dr. Cronus sighed and rolled his eyes. "And your aim is what? To make a million dollars?"

I nodded.

"Start with small steps," he said. "Every journey begins with the first step. That's my advice."

"Small steps."

"Yes. You need a plan. Do you have a notebook?"

"No."

Exasperated, Dr. Cronus produced one from his pocket. "Always carry paper. That's another piece of advice. You never know when a good idea might strike. Now. Think of some practical ways to make money. You could wash cars for neighbors on the weekends, that would be a start."

I looked down at my wrist. "Not going to be much use at that, am I?"

"Delegate. Get a team together. Now, come on, use your brain."

"Um . . . babysitting. People pay good money for that," I said.

"Excellent," said Dr. Cronus. "What else?"

"Um . . ."

We spent the next half hour coming up with ideas, and once we got going, I really got into it, and in the end we had a good list.

"When it seemed that we couldn't think of anything else, I read out the list. "Cake sale. Candle making. Guess games—like guess the number of candies or coins in a jar. Sponsored walks. Raffle tickets for donated prizes. Face painting. Rummage sale. These are really great ideas, but they'd only make peanuts. We'd raise some money, maybe enough to buy a piece of furniture, but never the whole wing. I need the big bucks."

"This would be a good start, and you have to start somewhere."

I had my doubts. It sounded like a lot of hard work for little return. Dr. Cronus seemed to pick up on my thoughts. "Impatient as usual. Always wanting everything to happen yesterday." He crossed his arms stubbornly. "See if I care. If you don't like my ideas, ask one of the others. That is why you have a zodiac phone, you know."

"It's not that I don't like your ideas, Dr. Cronus, but you're not thinking very ambitiously. This is a big project."

Angrily, the doctor challenged me. "Ask the others, then. See if I care."

"Well, Mario hasn't been much good. He keeps saying it has to come from me," I said.

Dr. Cronus gave the list a cursory glance. "These ideas did all come from you. Go on. Ask for help."

I pulled my phone out of my backpack and typed in the message:

```
Need help to raise big bucks.
```

I pressed SEND TO ALL.

My phone bleeped a few seconds later. It was Mario.

"You have two weeks left," he said. "You'd better get on with it."

"You are so impatient, Mario," I said. "Like, most people say, 'Hi, how are you?' when they pick up the phone."

"Hi, how are you, and what's your next step?" he asked.

"Um, I'm working on a plan and waiting for some input."

Dr. Cronus nodded and stroked his beard. Moments later, Uri appeared at the end of the concrete walkway that led across the park. He was on a skateboard and wearing his sci-fi costume again. He whizzed past us.

"Friends!" he called as he balanced on one leg. "New friends. Unite."

"Well, he would say that, wouldn't he?" Dr. Cronus muttered.

"Why would he?" I asked, as I watched Uri stand on his hands on the skateboard and go backward. He really was an excellent performer.

"Uri, Uranus. Rules Aquarius. Aquarians are big on friends and unity."

"So what did he mean? Oh, don't tell me, only I can

figure that out. Maybe that I have to apologize to Lois. I . . . I guess I can do that. In fact, I'll do it now!" I got out my regular phone and called Lois's cell phone. *With a bit of luck, she'll pick up on the bus,* I thought, as I listened to the dial tone.

"It's me," I said when she answered. "Please don't hang up. I'm sorry, Lois. I really am. I was a pig for making you spend all your money, and I'll make it up to you. When Mom gives me my next allowance, I'll repay you. Honest."

"No more scratch cards?"

"Heck no. They're for losers."

I heard Lois laugh on the other end of the phone. "Friends forever, right?"

"Deffo," I said. I hung up and gave Uri, who was whizzing past on one leg, a thumbs-up. "Fixed."

"Is Lois a new friend?" asked Dr. Cronus.

I shook my head. "No. We've know each other forever."

"If I'm not mistaken, Uri said new friends. So maybe not fixed. Oh, here comes Nessa." The beautician lady from the hospital appeared on the other side of the park. She was dressed in a white tracksuit and was jogging with her blond hair flowing out behind her.

"The right image will help," she said as she ran past.

I looked down at what I was wearing. I had on my usual jeans and a blue jacket. So? I was out on a cold gray fall day. What did she expect? A tiara? I put my hand up to my head. "Do you think she means my hair?"

Dr. Cronus looked at my head. "Very possibly."

"Do you mean my hair?" I called after her.

Nessa turned around and jogged back. She caught her breath and then took a good look at my hair, picking up strands and scrutinizing them critically. "Mmm. You have to do somethin' soon, darlin'. But you can't risk coloring again, not after what you did to it. It might all snap off. And . . . although your roots are coming through with new hair, there's not enough there yet to cut it short without you lookin' like you joined the marines. No, best to come into the salon one day, and I'll do a moisturizin' treatment on you, and we'll try to improve the condition. All right?"

I nodded. I knew that I looked weird—my red roots really stood out against the white color of the rest of my hair. I'd tried to tell myself that it was an individual look, but even I wasn't convinced. I pulled out my baseball cap from one of the pockets of my backpack.

"Cover up," I said as I put it on.

"Good idea, and it suits you," said Nessa, and off she jogged.

I turned to Dr. Cronus. "Hair advice wasn't exactly what I meant when I sent that text message that I wanted help."

"You have to be more specific, then," he replied.

Next came Selene. *Queen of the loons*, I thought, as she approached and I saw what she was wearing. She was dressed in a long silver-green ankle-length skirt and a blue silk top, and she had her silver-gray hair loose down her back. She beckoned to Nessa, who was now on the far side of the park. Nessa went over to her, and the two of them began to dance in the park. It was a strange dance that involved a lot of arm waving.

"What the . . . ?" I said. "They look like a pair of crazed hippies."

Dr. Cronus said, "Perhaps you should join them?"

"No chance," I said, holding up my cast. "I was up for a great part in the school play, you know, but because I hurt my arm, I can't be in it now. I think the school is prejudiced against people like me."

"Then why don't you tell them that?"

"Yeah right, don't think I didn't try. Actually . . ." an idea was starting to hatch in my head. "Hey, you may have something there."

Dr. Cronus sighed wearily. "At last!"

I didn't hear any more because I was up, on my way home. I had things to do. People to see. Speeches to write.

Chapter Seventeen

School assembly

I gazed out at the sea of faces in front of me and took a deep breath. *This is it,* I told myself. *My moment to change everything.* It was a Wednesday morning in the third week of my zodiac month, and Mr. Simpson, our principal, had given me some time at our school assembly after he'd made the usual announcements. *Stay calm,* I told myself. *And remember to speak slowly.* That was what our drama teacher had always told us about doing presentations—that and to be prepared. I figured that I was as ready as I was ever going to be, having spent every moment that I could since Saturday in the park with Dr. Cronus discussing what I was going to say. Plus I'd done a practice run-through on Monday evening and last night with Lois after school. I was confident that my speech would have the desired result. I'd worded and reworded it so many times. My plan was to appeal to everyone's conscience. A person would have to have a heart of stone not to be moved by what I had to say. I was going to get everyone onboard with the project to raise money for the new hospital wing. I'd realized while talking things over with Dr. C. that I couldn't do it on my own. It had to be a group effort involving everyone in the school. I'd coordinate it after I'd inspired everyone in front of me with what I had to say.

Mr. Simpson took off his glasses. "And now one of our students, Marsha Leibowitz from the seventh grade, has something that she'd like to say to you," he said, and he moved aside and indicated that I should step up to the podium. I took a deep breath and walked forward.

"Right. Hi, everyone. So, yeah. Around two weeks ago, I had a fall—as you can see." I held up my bandaged wrist, and someone at the back applauded. I didn't let her put me off and continued, "I hurt my wrist. I had to spend a couple of nights in the hospital. I can tell you it was a real eye opener—I'd never had to stay in one before. Anyway, what I wanted to say is, it got me thinking. It's very boring in there for a start—"

Halfway down the room, I could see a bunch of ninth-grade girls nudge each other; one rolled her eyes and another made a circular motion with her hand. I knew the gesture. It was one that I used when I thought someone was droning on and I wanted them to finish up. Seeing their reaction threw me off for a moment, and looking around the room, I could see that they weren't the only ones who looked uninterested. Quite a few people were looking out the windows or around at each other. "I . . . I am trying, that is, I am going to start a project, or . . . that is . . . a bunch of projects . . ." My confidence faltered, and my perfectly planned speech seemed to be deserting me. Suddenly, I felt cold inside and flat. *I am making a fool of myself*, I thought. *Everyone looks so bored, as if they can't wait for me to finish so they can get out into the hallway to talk to their friends.* I searched for Lois in the audience, and there she was in our usual spot, three fourths of the way back on the right. Her expression was concerned, but when she saw me look at her, she beamed and gave me the thumbs-up. *I can do this*, I told myself. *Don't give up now. I just have to make them listen.*

"I . . . Just try to imagine how you would feel if you had to go away from your home, away from what is familiar. It's not easy, I can tell you. The days and nights in a hospital can feel very long, especially for those who are in there long term." The girl who had been doing the finish-up gesture made a fist with her right hand, put it up to the corner of her eye, stuck out her bottom lip, and made a face like she was crying. Her friends loved it and did the same mock-crying act. *Just get through it*, I told myself. *Think of Amy.* "If there was a recreation wing for people in there, a place to go to relax and chill out and forget about illness and being sick and all the anxiety that goes with it, it would be so much easier. We are the people that can make that happen. I'm asking for your help. This Saturday from eleven o'clock onward, Mr. Simpson has given me—and anyone else who would like to volunteer—the use of the gym. We're going to have a fair to raise money. There will be all types of activities you can participate in. Cake sales. Guess the coins in a jar . . ."

I couldn't help but focus on the group of ninth-grade girls. They looked like they were about to have a giggling fit. The one who had rolled her eyes was now making silly faces, crossing her eyes and making a face like she was about to throw up. *Oh God, this isn't going well,* I thought. "Um. I've put up some forms on the bulletin board in the main hallway. Please sign up and, if you have any great ideas, put them down, too. Together we can make it happen."

I had meant to say the last part in a really enthusiastic voice. It was my slogan. I had put it on top of all the lists and was going to put it on any posters or leaflets. Together we can make it happen. But it came out in a whisper.

Mr. Simpson stepped forward. "Well done, Marsha. I like to hear that our students are participating in good causes."

The ninth-grade girl silently mimicked what Mr. Simpson had said, and her friends started giggling again, their shoulders shaking in silent laugher. I knew what they were thinking—that I was a Miss Goody Two-Shoes. That I was a bore. It was what I would have thought just a few weeks ago.

I stepped down from the stage and made my way over to Lois, keeping my eyes firmly down on the ground. This was one time I definitely did not want to be the center of attention.

Lois and I checked the lists on the bulletin board every break, every morning, and every afternoon until Friday. At first there were only a few names until a last check on Friday afternoon showed that the list had suddenly grown. A whole bunch of people had signed up.

"Hey, look at this, Lois," I said. "I knew people would come through in the end."

And then I read the names. Paris Hilton. Minnie Mouse. Betty Boop. Jessica Rabbit. Jane Eyre. Harry Potter. Professor Dumbledore. Winnie-the-Pooh. A whole list of fictional names.

"I bet I know who's done this, too," I said to Lois. "Those ninth-grade girls. Honestly, I'd like to see them spend a few days in the hospital with nothing to do. They wouldn't even last an hour."

Lois squeezed my arm. "Never mind. It's not over yet. I'm sure a few people will turn up tomorrow. I heard some seventh-grade girls in the locker room saying that they were going to come."

"And I'll send a text message to all my new planet friends to see if they will come along. As Mario keeps reminding me, I have just over a week left, and he did say that they are here to help."

"Together we can make it happen," said Lois. She put up her hand to high-five me.

I high-fived her back, but my heart was sinking.

Chapter Eighteen

Making it happen?

"I don't really see the point in even going," I said to Dad as we packed up the trunk of the car, ready to go to the gym. Dad put his arm around me and gave me a hug. "Come on, Marsha. This isn't like you. Where's that usual I-can-do-anything attitude of yours?"

Got up and died at the school assembly on Wednesday, I thought, as I remembered the mixed reception of laughter and boredom and then the fictional list.

Dad punched a fist into the air. "Together we can make it happen. Right?"

"Yeah," I said, and I stepped back from the car to do a karate leap and kick, if only to keep him happy. "I am the Zodiac Girl, huzzah!"

Dad laughed. "And what is that supposed to mean?"

"Me. Aries. According to an astrological website that Lois found, I am this month's Zodiac Girl."

"Great," said Dad. "Go, Zodiac Girl."

"Go," I said and smiled back at him. I didn't want to admit what a letdown it was going to be today. My family had been so amazing at supporting my venture that I felt embarrassed to tell them that no one was going to show up. Mom had spent the last two nights making some colorful posters to stick on the walls outside the school, and Dad had taken one of them to work and copied it so that we had a ton of leaflets to hand out. Mom had also been into the local thrift store and asked if they had any spare stuff. They told her to stop by early on Saturday morning, and they'd pile her car up high. They seemed glad for the chance to clear out their back room. Cissie and Eleanor had surpassed themselves and had spent the last few evenings baking a variety of cakes for the sale. By Saturday morning, they had a great mix of coffee, chocolate fudge, vanilla, and lemon cakes. They got into the back of the car with the goodies balanced on their knees. *Oh well,* I thought miserably, *at least we can eat the cakes.*

"I'll meet you there," said Mom, getting into her car.

"Do you have the balloons?" I asked as she started up the car.

She gave me a wave and a nod. "Check."

I got into the front of Dad's car, and he started up. As we drove off down the road, I gave myself a good talking to. *Get a grip, Marsha Leibowitz. You don't normally let things get to you. So what if not many people turn up? Lois and my family will be there, and you owe it to them to do your best.*

"Together we can make it happen," I said out loud.

"Yea!" chorused Dad, Cissie, and Eleanor.

Lois was already at the gym, along with a few of the teachers, when we got to school, and I was happy to see that Mrs. Pierson and Mr. Simpson were among them.

"Have to support my students in ventures like this," said Mr. Simpson. "Now, what would you like us to do?"

I beckoned him to come around to the back of the car, where Dad was unloading a big bowl and a pack of sponges. Mr. Simpson looked at me and then at the sponges and then back at me. He got what they were for right away.

"Oh, noooooo," he said with a groan.

I grinned back at him. "I was going to ask Dad to be the victim, but people will pay so much more to throw a wet sponge at their principal." *That's if anyone shows up*, said a voice in the back of my head.

Mrs. Pierson and Lois got busy blowing up balloons and then went outside to tie them to the railings, put up the posters, and give out leaflets to passersby. It was an hour until kickoff, and the streets were empty, aside from a car that had just pulled up outside the hall. Five young girls piled out.

"What do you want us to do?" asked a little blond one.

"We're here to help," added her redheaded, freckly friend.

"Take care of the rummage sale," I said, as Mom pulled up in her car. She got out and opened the trunk

157

to show us a ton of black garbage bags that looked ready to burst. "That would be great."

The girls set to it and were soon busy organizing their stall.

Inside the gym, Mrs. Pierson called me over to a table where she had set out four jars of homemade jam. "Not much to show," she said, "but you didn't give us much time."

"Oh, I think I can add to zat," said a man's voice, and we turned to see that Joe from the deli (the one who liked to play the Jupiter part) had arrived. He pointed out the window at the white van that he'd parked outside. "I need a few helping hands," he said. And when another group of seventh graders arrived, I sent them out to bring in Joe's contributions. Soon Mrs. Pierson's stall was groaning under the weight of all the food: pies, pastries, tarts, and delicious-looking baguettes stuffed with ham, cheese, and tomatoes.

"Hey, look," said Lois, as another group of girls arrived soon after. This time, the girls were eighth graders, including Carol Kennedy bearing bags of games and books.

"Left over from the Summer Fair," said Carol, as the girls began to display stuff on a table behind her. "Mr. Simpson told us to get it out of the supply cupboards."

"Thanks, Carol," I said.

Carol looked awkward for a moment and stared at the floor. "I wanted to do something to help. I knew how much the part of the Ice Queen meant to you and . . . well, I am sorry about what happened to you. It really stinks." She looked up from the floor and smiled. I smiled back.

"That means a lot," I said. "And good luck in the part. I'm sure you'll be really good."

Carol smiled. "I'll try my best, but I don't think I will be as good as you would have been."

I felt so touched by what she'd said. It was really generous of her. I would never have said anything like that to her if I'd been in her shoes. *People will never cease to surprise me*, I thought, as I watched her busy herself with all the others who had turned up to help.

After that, I hardly had time to think because everyone wanted to know what to do, where to set up, how much to charge for what. Luckily, Mario had arrived, and with Joe from the deli and Dad, he was soon organizing people to do various tasks, like setting up a coffee urn and pouring juice and water to go with the cakes and sandwiches. It was ten minutes to opening time, and the gym was a hive of activity, chatter, and laughter.

Nessa arrived with a couple of her assistants. She gave me a wink and then went off to set up a mini beauty salon in a corner of the gym. A board she put up showed that she was offering manicures, mini facials, and makeup sessions. I gave her the thumbs-up.

Next was Sophie King from tenth grade with one of her friends. She came right over. "Good for you, Marsha, for getting this organized."

I remembered the way I had brushed her off just before my accident, and I blushed. "I am so sorry about the way I acted, Sophie," I said. "You were trying to do your best to raise money, and I brushed you off. How did the show go?"

Sophie grimaced. "We had to cancel it in the end. I couldn't get anyone with any real talent to volunteer. Maybe I'll try another time, but it turned into a total nonstarter."

"But didn't you have a hall booked and everything?"

She nodded. "Yeah, for a week from today, in fact, but luckily I didn't lose the deposit because it was snapped up by a record company that is holding a dance competition. Apparently, their venue fell through at the last minute, so they were grateful to have somewhere to hold it."

"What type of dance?"

"Hip-hop. Cat Slick Moman is going to be judging it."

"*Cat Slick Moman?* The rapper?" I asked. I wondered if it was the competition that Skye should have been in. No wonder she was mad if Cat Slick Moman was judging it! He was mega.

"Yeah. There are going to be a whole lot of celebrities

160

there and Mr. Blake. You know—Oliver's dad."

"Michael Blake?"

"Yeah, he's Cat Slick's agent, apparently. Plus a whole bunch of his rapper friends will be there, too, because they're in town for some convention. Anyway, what do you want us to do?"

"Um . . ." I looked around the gym and saw that the glass jars Dad and I had filled with candy the night before were standing on a table nearby. "You could get the guess-how-many-candies-are-in-the-jar game started. Charge a dollar a guess, winner gets the whole jar."

"Will do," said Sophie, and she and her friend went off to get things started.

I glanced at my watch. "Five minutes till doors open!" I called.

"Ready!" called Lois from the coffee stall.

As I watched everyone take their places, I could feel a plan taking root, straining to burst into flower at the back of my mind. Something. Something—but I didn't have time to think about it any more because people were coming in the door. Even Dr. Cronus showed up to do his part and set himself up in a corner with a board advertising that he could give out homework tips. I gave him a wave, and he waved back.

The rest of the afternoon was a blur as more and more people arrived, and when it started raining at around

3:00 P.M., even more people came in, eager to find a cup of coffee, a dry place, and a bargain. I rushed around helping out where I could, sending out for supplies, more coffee, muffins to take the place of the cakes that had sold out, directing people toward the various stalls. We made a fortune on the game of throw a wet sponge at Mr. Simpson, who by 4:00 looked like a drowned rat.

When the doors closed at 4:30, all the volunteers sighed with relief. We sent Mr. Simpson home to take a bath and get warm, then Mom, Mrs. Pierson, and I collected all the money and went into the back room to add it up.

Dad brought us mugs of hot chocolate and a few pieces of carrot cake with cream cheese icing, which Cissie had saved for us, and we sat munching while Mom added up the figures.

"And the total is . . ." She looked around, delaying the moment.

"Oh, come on, Mom," I said with a groan.

"Five hundred and forty dollars and sixty-five cents exactly," she said.

"Yea," I said as everyone clapped.

"Excellent," said Mrs. Pierson. "That's more than we usually make at fundraisers. Well done, Marsha. Well done."

Okay, so it's not a million, I thought. *But it's a start.*

Chapter Nineteen

Skye

On the way home, I got Dad to drop me off at the hospital. I wanted to see Amy and let her know how the afternoon had gone. When I got to the room, I saw that she already had a visitor. Skye was by the side of the bed. She looked up and gave me a wave as I approached. Amy looked pale and tired and was lying back on her pillows. Nevertheless, her face brightened when she saw me.

"Hi, Marsha," she said.

"Hi. How you doing?"

"Same old. You?"

I held up my arm. "It's itching like crazy. Can't wait to get it off."

Skye looked down at her foot. "Me, too," she said. "I feel like I want to put a stick inside the cast and scratch it."

"Hey, a girl from my school told me about that competition you were going to be in. Cat Slick Moman's judging?"

Skye grimaced and looked back at her foot. "Yeah.

163

Bummer. I'll still go to watch, but it's going to be hard now that I can't perform. I had a great routine worked out and all, and then this had to happen."

"I know how you feel. I was supposed to play the part of the Ice Queen in our school play. I worked really hard to get it, too." I indicated my hair. "Even dyed my hair for the part."

Skye laughed and shot Amy a conspiratorial look. "We wondered."

"I know. It looks really weird. I'll have it cut soon. It just needs to grow a little first."

Skye stared at my head. "You know, it would look really cool if you had it cut short, but spiked it up, keeping the roots red and the tips white. It would be totally unique."

"Crazy, more like," I said. "I hardly take my baseball cap off these days."

"Show me your routines," said Amy.

"*Our routines?*" I asked.

Amy nodded. "Yeah. Your dance routines."

Skye laughed. "Yeah, right."

I held up my arm. "Um, slightly out of action at the moment," I said.

"Says who? Oh, come on," said Amy. "Do them for me. I don't have to tell you how boring it is being in here in bed all day with nothing to look at but the ceiling. I loved watching you dance last time you were here."

Skye and I exchanged glances, and then she nodded. "Okay. But, Marsha, you go first."

"But I have no music," I said.

Skye began to slow clap, and Amy joined in. *Clap, clap, clap.*

"Oh, all right," I said, and I stood up. "Okay. Um . . . You have to imagine that it's winter. All the trees are covered in snow. And you are lost in the woods." I turned my back, made myself get into the character of the Ice Queen, cold-hearted and royal, then I turned around and went into my routine. At first I felt awkward with my arm strapped up, but after a while I got into it, and as the steps came back, it didn't seem to matter. I glanced over at Skye and Amy. Amy looked transfixed, and even Skye looked impressed. When I finished, I sat back down on the end of the bed. "I know. Terrible. It's hard to do it with my arm all strapped up."

Skye shook her head. "No. No. You're really good, Marsha. Really good."

"Yeah," said Amy. "You can see that you have a natural talent. That was awesome."

I felt incredibly flattered and grinned back at her. "You're just saying that."

"No, I'm not," said Amy.

I looked at Skye. "Okay. You're next."

Skye took a deep breath and heaved herself up. "Ha,"

she said. "This is going to be such a mess, hip-hop like you've never seen it before. Um. Okay . . ."

She began to hum a rhythm, which I soon picked up, and Amy and I began to clap in time as Skye went into her routine. It didn't matter that her foot was strapped up and her movements were limited. Anyone could see by the way she moved her upper body that she could dance, and she had great attitude, like laid-back but cool and sharp.

She finished by doing a slow swirl with her crutches and then gave a short bow. Amy and I clapped and clapped. "Skye, you were fantastic. Really good. You easily would have won if you were in that competition," said Amy.

Skye sighed. "Maybe."

"There will be other competitions. You can enter them," I said.

"Yeah. Right back at 'ya. There will be other plays."

I sighed. "Not with guys like Michael Blake and Cat Slick in the audience."

Just at that moment, my zodiac phone bleeped that I had a message. It was from Mario.

```
Uri said to remind you about new friends.
```

I looked over at Amy and Skye and texted back.

```
Yeah. I have new friends.
```

He texted right back.

```
New friends unite.
```

"Another riddle," I said and showed the girls my phone. "Remember I told you that I won this phone? Well, the guy that runs the website keeps sending me mysterious messages. Like new friends—I guess that means you two—but new friends unite. What does that mean?"

Skye shrugged, but Amy's eyes shone. "I know. I bet I know," she said. "Like what were we just talking about?"

"The show that Skye was in," I replied.

"Missed opportunities," said Skye.

"That's just it," said Amy. "Are they all solo performances in the competition?"

Skye shook her head. "No, there are all sorts of entries, solo, duos, groups."

"Duos, groups," repeated Amy.

Skye gave her a puzzled look and then nodded as if she'd understood something. "Oh, I think I see where you're going. No. Come on."

"What?" I asked, and then it dawned on me, too.

Amy nodded. "You have the feet, Marsha; Skye has the arms and the crutches. You can both dance. Oh, come on. You have to do it."

I glanced at Skye.

"No way. We'd look insane. The people who enter these competitions are in a different league. We'd be wasting our time."

"Chicken," said Amy.

"*Chicken?* I am not. You don't know what it's like," said Skye.

"I know that life is short," said Amy. "I know that sometimes you have to go for it, even when everything seems set against you. What do you have to lose? What do you think, Marsha?"

"I . . . I . . ." I glanced over at Skye. "I think Amy's right, Skye. What do we have to lose? And, if nothing else, we can draw attention to the fact that the hospital needs funds for the new wing."

The beginning of a smile was breaking at the corner of Skye's mouth. "You and me?"

"Yeah. And . . ." I suddenly had the most amazing idea. "Not just us. I have a few friends who may help out, too. Friends who have always wanted to dance. So, yeah. I say, let's do it. You in?"

Skye nodded. "Nothing ventured, et cetera, et cetera."

"And, if I'm feeling better," said Amy, "I want to come. If this stint in the hospital has taught me anything, it's that life is too short to sit around moping when you could be out hip-hopping."

She put up her hand to high-five us.

Chapter Twenty

Auditions

"So who are these other friends?" asked Skye when we got outside of the hospital after visiting Amy.

"My zodiac buddies. Remember the phone I won? Well, another part of the prize was that I got the help of these people who um . . . How can I explain it? I think that they're part of a club that likes dressing up, you know? Only they don't exactly dress up, they um . . . pretend to be characters. Oh, I'm not explaining it very well. Like some people join clubs where they dress up as characters out of books, other people dress up as knights of old and relive battle scenes, well the zodiac people all pick a planet to be. Something like that."

Skye raised an eyebrow. "They sound crazy," she said.

"Yeah, that's what I thought, but they're okay. Like that clown doctor—he's one of them."

"Oh, him? He was good," said Skye. "Yeah, I liked him."

"And the lady that did the pampering sessions, she's another one."

"Yeah, she was okay," said Skye.

"Well, I was thinking, I only have another week of their help, so why not get them into our group, too? It would be pretty cool if you and I were out front, but we had this back-up group behind us doing some cool dance steps."

Skye considered the idea. "Yeah, maybe, but we have a heck of a lot to do in one week, like the choreography—"

I thought back to seeing Selene and Nessa dancing in the park. "They like to dance, and I've seen a few of them move. And we have to decide what to wear, don't you think? Like, should we all wear the same thing or dress individually?"

"Same thing," said Skye. "Always looks slicker. And, jeez, we need a rap song. We'll never do it in time."

"I have the start of one already. It started in my head when we were up in the ward. I thought we could do it about the hospital."

Skye didn't look enthusiastic. "Maybe, but who wants to hear about being in the hospital?"

"Let's give it a try," I said, and I began to rap.

"You'd have to be a dummy
To find the hospital funny.
Ain't no joke. Choke back a tear.
Don't wanna be here."

Skye put her head to one side and grinned at me. "Hey, newbie, that's not bad. You just thought that up? Yeah. I like it." She started moving her arms and crutches crisscross as she sang my words. "Hey, it's okay. Yeah."

"So if we only have a week, we should start right away, right?"

Skye nodded. "And I think we should start by seeing your new friends. See if they really can dance."

"Good plan," I said, and I pulled out my phone. I typed in a message.

```
Calling all planets. Now is your chance to
dance. Auditions at . . .
```

"Hey, where should we have the auditions? I don't want to take them back to my house. My parents and sisters will want to butt in and be in the group, too." I finished the text message:

```
. . . the park in Osbury in one hour.
```

"Ditto. Families, huh? Always want to know what you're up to."

"I said the park in Osbury," I replied. "It's a good space there, and the sky is clear."

Skye nodded. "Lead on."

Dr. Cronus was already there by the time the bus that Skye and I had caught from the hospital arrived. He was dressed in a long cloak that covered him from tip to toe.

"Who's the old guy?" asked Skye, as I gave him a wave.

"He's actually the principal at a local private school, but in the zodiac game he plays Saturn."

"So what's Saturn?"

"The taskmaster of the zodiac, so I guess it fits that he's a principal."

Skye giggled. "Yeah, but can he dance?"

"We'll see," I replied. "Everyone has their chance."

"Yeah," said Skye. "This is so cool. It's like we're going to be the judges on one of those reality, looking-for-talent shows."

"Yeah," I said. "I've always wanted to do that. We should have buzzers."

As we made our way over to Dr. Cronus, I saw that Uri was coming over on his unicycle.

"There's the clown doctor—Hey!" called Skye.

Uri stood on the seat of his cycle and did a comedy wave like the Queen of England does. Behind him, I saw that Mario was coming, accompanied by Nessa, the beautician lady.

I leaned into Skye's ear and whispered, "The clown doctor is Uri for Uranus, and the hunky black guy is Mario for Mars, and the lady is Nessa for Venus."

"She is beautiful. Should you and I pick planets to be?"

"Um, I don't think it works like that."

"We have to pick a name for our group, though," said Skye.

I nodded. "Yeah. But let's see who's in it first."

Mario caught up with us and gave Skye a nod. "So. Auditions? Marsha, what's this about?"

"I'll tell you." With Skye's help, I got up on a park bench. "Okay, gather around, everyone. We've had another idea about how to raise money for the recreation wing at the hospital. There's a competition next Saturday night." I pointed across the park. "It's being held in the community center over there, and there are going to be some very important people there. Celebrities, agents, but, most importantly, the prize is ten thousand dollars. I know it's not a million and that's what I was hoping to raise, but it's a good start."

Everyone nodded as if they approved.

"My friend Skye and I are getting a group together. The type of dance is hip-hop. If you want to audition, get in line."

All the planet people started pushing and shoving to be first in line. Dr. Cronus was the worst of all.

"Hey, hey!" I called. "That's no way to behave. Okay, Dr. Cronus, if you're so desperate, you can go first, but stop shoving."

173

The planet people looked sheepish, but they did as they were told.

Skye sat on the bench, and I pulled Mario aside. "I thought that there were ten of you planets? I have ten names listed in my phone. Why haven't I met all of you, and why isn't the whole group here?"

"It depends on the individual chart," Mario replied. "It depends on which planets are strongly aspected in your chart during the time you are a Zodiac Girl. Some Zodiac Girls meet some of the planets, some meet the others. Everyone here today is here because they are prevalent in your chart. In fact, Jupiter should be along in a moment."

"You mean Joe, the deli man?"

Mario nodded, and indeed Joe's tubby figure was soon seen puffing his way across the park. He arrived with a big grin and a basket of goodies, which he proceeded to hand out.

"A troupe can't dance on an empty stomach," he said and passed me a ham and cheese sandwich.

"Let's get a move on!" Skye called from the bench. "It's going to be dark soon. If it's not your turn, please sit down. Dr. Cronus, when you're ready."

Dr. Cronus turned his back to us and then flung off his cloak with a dramatic gesture. He turned around. I felt my mouth fall open, and I desperately had to resist the urge to laugh. I didn't dare to look at Skye in case I did.

Dr. Cronus was wearing lycra danc shorts and ballet shoes. He stood up on his toes, did a pirouette, and then danced away. He did look funny, because he was very skinny and had the knobbliest knees I had ever seen, but he was light on his feet and very graceful. He did a leap to his left, spun around, and ended with a deep bow. We all clapped, and he almost smiled as he picked up his cloak and sat down with the others.

I leaned over to Skye. "What do you think?"

"Um, it's not exactly hip-hop, but the old guy can move. What do you think?"

"We could give him a chance. Explain that it's a different style of dance from his audition, but I think we should let him join us. He'd be so upset if we turned him down."

Skye nodded. "My thoughts, too, and our group is about giving a chance to people who might not have one."

"Exactly," I said and then called, "Next!"

Joe got up and he beckoned to Nessa to join him. They put their arms around each other like old-fashioned dancers and danced a waltz.

"Nice, but nothing special," I commented to Skye, and she nodded back at me.

When they had finished, they did low bows. "Um, thank you," I said. "We'll let you know." The enthusiasm that I'd felt earlier was beginning to fade. We would be a laughing stock. A bunch of fools. Two girls with injuries, an old timer with skinny legs and knobbly knees, and a couple who belonged in the 1930s. *Oh well,* I thought, *I doubt if Uri and Mario can be any worse.*

"Next!" I called.

Mario got up. He had brought a CD player with him. He pressed START, and some rap music began to play. Skye and I clapped along as he began his steps, leading first with his right elbow and then his shoulder. He was absolutely amazing, as good as any of the dancers I'd seen on TV. Halfway through the routine, he did splits and then he bounced up as if he were made of rubber. He sprang down lightly onto his hands and danced while doing a handstand.

"Ohmigod," said Skye, while Mario stood on his head and spun around. We were about to start clapping when he got up, ready to do a few more steps. Uri got up and began to dance with him in perfect time, perfectly in the beat, perfectly in sync. They had rhythm, they had attitude, they had charisma.

"Who are these guys?" asked Skye.

I shrugged. "Dunno. They're really good, though, aren't they?"

"Awesome," said Skye. "The best. We could win with them on our side."

I grinned back at her. "I know."

Chapter Twenty-one

Preparation

"What do we have so far?" asked Skye.

We were sitting on either side of Amy's bed, working on the rap song with her after school. Amy was looking good today, with more color in her cheeks, and was proving to be a whiz at writing songs.

Skye read from the pad of paper in front of her.

"LEDs twinklin',
People sleepin',
Heavy breathin',
Tubes a leakin',
High-tech bleepin'."

She nodded. "Okay, what next?"
"Try this," said Amy.

"Me silently freakin'.
I want to scream out,
But I know I can't shout.

I'm stuck here alone,
Just want to go home."

"Incredible," said Skye. "You're really good at this, Amy. Okay. Chorus."

"You'd have to be a dummy to find the hospital funny," we all sang. "Ain't no joke. Choke back a tear. Don't wanna be here."

Amy smiled. "It's sounding good. How are the rehearsals going?"

Skye laughed. "Aside from Mario and Uri, it's like trying to teach a bunch of kindergarten kids, but they'll get there. The routine is really simple."

"And it's going to look so good with all of us doing it if everyone can stay in time," I said. "Course, my sisters got wind of it and insisted on being in it, too, and my friend Lois didn't want to be left out, so the group is growing."

"What are you all going to wear?" asked Amy.

"Nessa's figuring that out," said Skye. "She's the beauty lady who came in, remember? She said she could get them for us in bulk, so we'll see tonight."

"Yeah. We're meeting every night after school because we don't have long to get it together," I said. "So, come on, we need another verse. Um . . . how about . . . um . . . Whispers comin' down the hall—"

"Yeah, good," said Skye. "And shadows slidin' on the wall—"

"An emergency," Amy added. "Thank God it ain't me. Some kid's fighting for life—"

"Me, I got no strife," said Skye.

"Just feelin' scared," said Amy. "Wish somebody cared. We may be sick—"

We were all quiet for a few moments.

"But when all's said an' done," I continued, "we still need some fun."

"And chorus," said Skye, and she began to snap her fingers in time.

"You'd have to be a dummy to find the hospital funny," we all sang. "Ain't no joke. Choke back a tear. Don't wanna be here."

"Yea," I said when we'd finished. "Read back that last verse, Skye."

"Whispers comin' down the hall," she read.
"Shadows slidin' on the wall,
An emergency.
Thank God it ain't me.
Some kid's fighting for life.
Me, I got no strife,
Just feelin' scared,
Wish somebody cared.

We may be sick. But when all's said an' done,
We still need some fun."

"Sounds great to me," I said. "Well done, team.
Another verse, and I think we're just about there."

After our visit with Amy, Dad drove me and Skye to the
community center in Osbury where the competition was
going to be held. Luckily for us, Mario had the keys
because he taught a self-defense class there a couple of
nights a week. The whole crew was there. Dr. Cronus
(who mercifully was dressed normally this time in pants
and a shirt), Joe the deli man, Nessa, Uri, Lois, Cissie, and
Eleanor were waiting for us with one new addition:
Nurse Cheryl.

"When Amy told me about this, I just had to come.
Is it okay?" she asked.

"*Okay?* It's fantastic," said Skye. "So, everybody
ready?"

Everyone nodded, so Skye hobbled over to a CD
player in the corner and put in a CD. Seconds later, the
room filled with the sound of hip-hop music.

She indicated her foot and her crutch. "Okay, so you
all have to be patient with me," she said. "We have our
own song, but the CD will give us the backbeat, and then
Marsha and I will do our hospital rap over it. Okay. I'll

run through it, then just follow what Marsha and I do."

She began to march in place "Okay. Everyone, just march, bend your knees, keep it loose. Right, now walk forward, tap, then back."

Everyone did as she said.

"Now we're going to add some arms. As you walk forward, lift your arms, push out with your elbows leading, one two three, alternate elbows out as if you're jostling someone aside with your elbows. That's it, good. Forward. Now when we go back, I want you to put your palm to the opposite shoulder as if you're wiping it and turn your face to the shoulder as you do so. Excellent. Looking good."

It wasn't looking good. No one was in time. Some were wiping when they should be nudging with their elbows.

Skye wasn't put off by the mess in front of her. She persevered. We marched forward, jumped back, arms thrown away, crossed. It looked good when she did it, even with her cast on.

"Attitude, attitude!" Skye yelled at us. "Dr. Cronus, you look way too uptight. Go for a cross between you couldn't care less and don't mess with me. Perfect, Uri. Perfect, Mario."

We stepped to the right, tapped, stepped to the left, again throwing arms forward in a gesture as if to say, I can't be bothered. I almost got the giggles at one point when I glanced over at Dr. Cronus. He was following the steps so earnestly but kept missing the beat and marching when he should have been jumping and throwing his arms whenever he could.

"Okay, last half," said Skye, "then we repeat, repeat, repeat. Walk forward, always starting on the right foot, one two three. Now put your hands on your hips, like you're tucking your thumbs into the tops of your pants, then back you go, turning your body sideways. Right, now forward again, this time slide to the right, to the left, good. Looking good. Let's take it from the top."

We went over and over the steps. Slowly, slowly, everyone caught on, and for a few brief seconds here and there, I got a glimpse of how it might look if everyone kept it together.

And then Dr. Cronus decided that he wanted to do a solo piece. He sprang onto his hands as if he was going to try break dancing, cried out in pain, and crumpled in a heap on the floor.

"Oops," I said, as Nurse Cheryl ran forward to see if he'd hurt himself.

Chapter Twenty-two

Showtime

It was the night of the competition.

We were to be on last.

Our crew sat in the audience with the other contestants and their friends and families to watch the performers. We took our seats, and the air was buzzing with anticipation and chatter.

Skye nudged me. "Ohmigod," she said. "He's here."

I turned to see that Cat Slick Moman had just arrived or, should I say, made his entrance. The door burst open, and in he came with an entourage of glamorous people behind him. He was dressed in black, had a black bandana on his head, and was wearing sunglasses, even though it was dark outside. He stopped at the door as if giving us all time to have a good look at him. And we did. Everyone stared. Behind him were two huge bodyguards who looked like heavyweight wrestlers. They were wearing fancy dark suits and also had sunglasses on, which they both took off at the same time as they stared around the audience, looking for anyone suspicious. Next came two pairs of twins who walked up to Cat Slick, and one of each linked his arm in a manner that suggested that we could look but not touch. One pair of twins were blond Barbie types dressed in pink tracksuits, the other pair were dark skinned and dressed in black. None had a flicker of a smile. *Now that's the attitude that Skye was talking about*, I thought, as I took in the expressions on their faces and the way that they jutted out one hip.

"I wouldn't like to meet them on a dark night," I said.

"Yeah. They look like tough cookies," said Skye. "But I bet it's all an act, like my cool act."

I looked at her for a moment, and her face broke into a grin. I grinned back at her and squeezed her arm with my good hand.

Cat Slick Moman and his entourage seemed to glide across the floor to the front, where they took seats. Cat nodded at Michael Blake who had arrived five minutes earlier with his son, Ollie. Everyone in the hall was staring at their every move, taking in every gesture— me included. I'd never been so close to a real live celebrity before.

"This is so exciting," said Lois as she looked around the hall.

"I know," I said. "And Ollie Blake . . ."

"Swoon, swoon," we chorused.

". . . keeps looking over," I finished.

After Cat, a few more famous rappers arrived, DJ Diggie and Ice Pick Pete. They sloped forward and sat in the front. Just looking at them was giving me butterflies. I couldn't believe that in around half an hour I was going to have to get up and perform in front of them!

The show swiftly started once everyone was seated and the lights went down. The first act was a boy who looked around 15. He was dressed in the usual baggy clothes that were fashionable for hip-hop back in the 1980s. His music started up, and he began to dance. He was good, very good, and Skye and I exchanged anxious glances.

Next up was a group of three black girls, and they were completely amazing, as if they were made of Jell-O, and they ended their act by doing splits. I glanced over at Dr. Cronus, who had his arm in a sling and hoped that the girls weren't giving him any ideas about trying to do a split himself. He gave a slight wave with his good hand and grimaced. I was growing fond of Dr. C. He might be Saturn and a principal, but he was a trooper.

A few other groups of girls followed, and they were all good, but, as the evening progressed, I didn't feel that anyone stood out. They could all dance, but there was nothing unique about any of them.

"I think we might have a chance because we're different," I whispered to Skye.

"Yeah," she whispered back and then giggled. "You can say that again. And, hey, Cheryl hasn't shown up."

"Maybe she chickened out," I said. "Or didn't want to be associated with us. I wouldn't blame her."

After an hour, there was a short break for refreshments, and I noticed that one of Cat Slick's bodyguards opened up a huge freezer box and handed out bottles of juice to the entourage. I'd read somewhere that Cat Slick was anti-booze and only drank organic juice.

"We'd better go backstage and get dressed," said Cissie. "Nessa has our outfits ready."

I got up to go, and as I did, Skye nudged me again. I noticed that someone was coming in the door at the back. "Hey!" I called when I saw who it was. It was Amy and she was with Nurse Cheryl, who was pushing Amy's wheelchair. Her mom and dad were behind her, and Nurse Cheryl waved when she saw us.

"We're not too late, are we?" she asked when they reached us.

"You've missed the first half, but there are loads of others to go," I said and indicated where Skye and I had been sitting. "Here. Take our places."

Amy's mom stepped forward at this point. She looked so much like Amy, with the same brown hair and fine features. "Actually," she said. "We were hoping that Amy could be onstage with you. I know she's in her wheelchair, but maybe she could do the rap song with you."

I glanced at Skye, who nodded.

"Course," I said. "Yeah. That would be great."

"Great," said Cheryl. "So let's get ready to boogie."

Backstage, all our crew was changing into the outfits that Nessa had chosen for us. They were perfect: baggy white tracksuits with a silver stripe up the side of the legs and the arms, white baseball caps—which we all wore backward—and humongous white sneakers.

"Hey, Dr. C.," I said when I saw him checking himself out in the mirror. "You look way cool."

He nodded and turned his baseball cap backward. "Yes, I do."

"And one last touch," said Nessa when we were almost ready. We all burst out laughing when she produced bandages, slings, and eye patches. "Help yourselves, guys."

Everyone fell upon the "accessories." Mario went for an eye patch, which suited him. Uri went for a bandage that he wound around his middle in a bizarre way, but I was starting to get that that was his personality. Nessa bandaged her head, and Joe the deli man went for a leg cast and a crutch. Amy went for an arm bandage, and my sisters both picked eye patches. I think that they wanted to be like Mario—they kept glancing at him and giving him flirty looks. Once we were all dressed and

187

ready, we looked like a bunch of crazies.

"Okay, let's go," I said, and we left the dressing room and gathered in the wings of the stage, along with the other waiting contestants. Skye looked around at our group and got the giggles and that started me off and that started Amy off, and soon all of us were holding our sides laughing.

"Shh," said the MC, so I did my best to straighten my face and focus on the stage. A group of four boys was springing around on their hands, just finishing.

"We can't compete with that," said Skye.

"Well, Mario and Uri can," I said. "No problem."

As we stood waiting for the stage to clear, I stared out into the audience. My butterflies were all up and flying around inside me like they were trying to escape. Cat Slick and his friends looked completely unimpressed, their faces giving away nothing, although they clapped politely at the end of each performance.

"And now for our last act," said the lady, who was the event's MC. "A new group, and I'm told that, if they win, they want to donate the proceeds to build a new recreation wing at our local hospital. So let's put our hands together for Accident Prone." The name had come to me early this morning, and when I suggested it to the others, everyone loved it.

We hobbled onto the stage like a bunch of invalids who

could hardly move, and the audience began to cheer as we took our positions. Amy took her place to the right of the stage, and Dad gave the nod and turned on the CD player. The beat started up. We began to tap our feet and then faced the audience and went into our routine.

Walk forward one two three, back, right elbow up and out left, up and out, right up and out. So far, so good. We were all in sync.

As the crew fell into step behind us, Skye and I stepped forward, and Amy wheeled herself over to join us. We went into our rap, and I glanced over at Cat Slick. For a moment I almost lost my concentration because he had taken his glasses off, was sitting up straight, and had a big smile on his face. Next to him, Ollie Blake was watching me, and he was smiling, too.

"LEDs twinklin',
People sleepin',
Heavy breathin',
Tubes a-leakin',
High-tech bleepin',
Me silently freakin'.
I want to scream out,
But I know I can't shout.
I'm stuck here alone,
Just want to go home," rapped Amy.

We all joined in with,
"You'd have to be a dummy
To find the hospital funny.
Ain't no joke. Choke back a tear.
Don't wanna be here."

Skye and I fell into step with the others. They were doing amazingly. Even though we'd rehearsed every night since we'd decided to enter the competition, I'd still had my doubts and wondered if it was going to be a major disaster. But everyone seemed to be totally together. As agreed, halfway through we all stood back and let Uri and Mario come forward. They did their handsprings and head spins, and the audience cheered. They loved them. We were about to fall back in when Dr. Cronus stepped forward. *Oh God, I hope he's not going to ruin everything*, I thought, as the old man kneeled on the floor and attempted to stand on his head. One attempt, and he fell back, a second, and he lost his balance and then . . . he was up! Spinning! The audience roared their appreciation. He sprang up like a 15-year-old, grinning from ear to ear, his sore wrist magically healed, then his knee gave way, and he had to hobble back into line. The audience thought that it was part of the act and laughed.

We fell back in step, got to the end of the rap, and by the last chorus, Cat was on his feet rapping the chorus with us. The audience clapped along. People at the back stood. I looked over at Amy and Skye and gave them the thumbs-up.

We went into the last steps, forward one two three, bend the knees, wiggle through the body, make a half circle with the right arm, step touch to the left, step touch to the right, and we were done.

The wait at the end felt like eternity, but finally the MC stepped up.

"And third place goes to Arthur C."

The audience clapped as the first boy got up and took his prize.

"And, in second place, Biz Gos and the Goose Girlies."

The three girls who did splits took to the stage.

"And, in first place . . ." She held her breath, and I held mine. "First place goes to . . . Accident Prone!"

The place erupted, and everyone got onto their feet, including Cat Slick Moman.

We climbed and hobbled up onto the stage and took our bows. *This is one of the best moments of my whole life*, I thought, as I looked out at the cheering crowd and then at my fellow dancers. It couldn't have been more perfect, even if I'd played the Ice Queen. It was better than that because, although I was center stage, I was there with the team, and it felt so good to share it.

Epilogue

A month after the competition, Cat Slick Moman released a new single. It was called "Hospital Rap" and was written by three girls, Amy, Skye, and Marsha. It went straight to number one in the charts and raised two million dollars. The girls gave the proceeds to Osbury General Hospital. Building work on the recreation wing for children and teenagers in the hospital started soon after.

Amy, Skye, and Marsha were booked to cut the ribbon on the opening day. By that time, Marsha's hair was back to normal.

Hospital Rap

LEDs twinklin',
People sleepin',
Heavy breathin',
Tubes a-leakin',
High-tech bleepin',

Me silently freakin'.
I want to scream out,
But I know I can't shout.
I'm stuck here alone,
Just want to go home.

You'd have to be a dummy
To find the hospital funny.
Ain't no joke. Choke back a tear.
Don't wanna be here.

Whispers comin' down the hall,
Shadows slidin' on the wall,
An emergency.
Thank God it ain't me.
Some kid's fighting for life.
Me, I got no strife,
Just feelin' scared,
Wish somebody cared.
We may be sick,
But when all's said an' done,
We still need some fun.

You'd have to be a dummy
To find the hospital funny.
Ain't no joke. Choke back a tear.

Don't wanna be here.
Gonna put on a show,
That's the way to go,
Find some folks with cash,
Raise a real big stash
And build a palace of fun
For everyone.
So 'stead of lying around,
Wearin' a frown,
Kids have a place of their own,
A leisure zone,
Some real home from home
To hang out and chill,
Forget that they're ill.

'Cause you'd have to be a dummy
To find the hospital funny.
Ain't no joke.

The Aries Files

Characteristics, Facts and Fun

March 21—April 20

Confident, daring, and spontaneous, Arians are always looking for new challenges. They are natural-born leaders and are at their happiest when they can show everyone what they're good at!

An Aries who's not getting her way can be impatient and stroppy, but they make brilliant friends. If you're feeling bored, energetic Aries will always think of something exciting to do!

Element:	Fire
Color:	Red
Birthstone:	Diamond
Animal:	Ram
Lucky day:	Tuesday
Planet:	Ruled by Mars

An Arian's best friends are likely to be:
Sagittarius
Leo

An Arian's enemies are likely to be:
Cancer
Libra

An Arian's idea of heaven would be:
Being the center of attention, like the lead in the school play!

An Arian would go crazy if:
They were being bossed around by someone—teachers beware!

Marsha's Top Audition Tips

1. **Know yourself!** Choose a character or part that you can identify with, and acting will be easy!

2. **Practice makes perfect!** You HAVE to know your piece by heart. Don't look at the words unless you go completely blank.

3. **Stand out!** If you wear a bright color or pattern to the audition, you will be remembered, but make sure it's something comfortable. Try not to look too crazy though . . .

4. **Be confident!** But not full of yourself. Nobody

likes a diva!

5. **Smile!** It will make people think that you are fun to work with, and it's harder to be nervous when you smile.

6. **Keep going!** Don't make a big deal if you make a mistake, and no one will notice.

Are you a typical Aries?

You're at school and you notice a younger kid being picked on. What do you do?
A) It's none of your business, so you keep out of it.
B) Go over to him later and teach him how to stand up for himself.
C) March over there and stand up for him. You can't tolerate bullies.

You've gone to see a movie you've wanted to see for ages. Someone is talking in the row behind you. What do you do?
A) Change seats.
B) Complain to the manager.
C) Turn around and give them a piece of your mind! Shu-ut UP!!!

You're having a party and no one's dancing! What do you do?
A) Try to persuade your best friends to get on the dance floor.
B) Decide that your party is a failure and have a tantrum.
C) Jump on the dance floor and show everyone

your latest moves. You love to show off!

You go shopping for a great party outfit. What do you choose?
A) Something simple, classic and black. You can't go wrong with that!
B) Whatever is the height of fashion. You wouldn't be caught dead in anything else.
C) Something wild to get you noticed—in the brightest color possible. You can start a new trend.

Your mom and dad have finally given in and said you can have a pet. What do you go for?
A) A puppy—you want something loyal and cuddly.
B) A kitten—like you, it's independent and strong-willed.
C) A snake—you'll be the talk of the school!

You see a group of girls in the cafeteria chatting and looking over at you. What do you think?
A) They are just having a chat and looking around to see who is there.
B) They are probably talking about some TV program they saw last night.
C) They are talking about you. Doesn't everyone?

How did you score?

Mostly As—almost Aries
Your Aries personality is in there somewhere; you just need to let it out . . .

Mostly Bs—agreeably Aries
You've got loads of great Aries qualities—don't be afraid to show them off!

Mostly Cs—amazingly Aries
Wow—you know what you want and you know how to get it! You're Aries to a T.

Zodiac Girls by Cathy Hopkins

Every month a Zodiac Girl is chosen, and for that month the planets give her advice. When will *your* sign shine?

Brat Princess
Leo

Star Child
Virgo

Discount Diva
Taurus

From Geek to Goddess
Gemini

Recipe for Rebellion
Sagittarius